Morse Hamilton

THE GARDEN OF EDEN MOTEL

Greenwillow Books
New York

The text of this book is set in Times Roman.

Printed in the United States of America

First Edition   10 9 8 7 6 5 4 3 2 1

Library of Congress Cataloging-in-Publication Data

Hamilton, Morse.

The Garden of Eden Motel / by Morse Hamilton.

    p.   cm.

Summary: In the early 1950s, eleven-year-old Dal accompanies
his stepfather, Mr. Sabatini, on a business trip to a rural
community in Idaho, where Dal makes new friends and
becomes involved in a scheme involving a uranium mine.

ISBN 0-688-16814-0   [1. Stepfathers—Fiction.

2. Country life—Idaho—Fiction.   3. Idaho—Fiction.

4. Uranium mines and mining—Fiction.]   I. Title.

PZ7.H18265Gar   1999   [Fic]—dc21

98-46684   CIP   AC

FOR ABBY

CONTENTS

THE TRAIN

"I wouldn't do that if I was you," said the man in the checkered suit. He was sitting by himself at a table for four in the crowded dining car, smearing stinky cheese on bits of roll.

Hands on hips, feet wide apart, Dal was trying to keep his balance without holding on as the Detroit–Chicago train went speeding around a long curve: *chucka-chucka-cha, chucka-chucka-cha.* He didn't have to obey a stranger, did he? He looked over his shoulder at Mr. Sabatini to make sure. "He's right," Mr. Sabatini said, gripping the back of an empty chair. "You don't want to crack your head open."

Brother, Dal thought. Is this what it's like to have a stepfather?

Just then the engineer must have tapped lightly on the brakes because the whole car shuddered, long enough for Dal to stumble sideways and, sure enough, bang his forehead—*boink*—against the thick plate glass window. (Didn't hurt, though.)

"Can't say we didn't warn you," said Mr. Sabatini cheerfully, while the man in the checkered suit licked his fingers and laughed.

Dal put one hand lightly on the edge of the man's table, but only until the train found its rhythm again: *chucka-chucka-cha, chucka-chucka-cha.* Then he held on with just his feet again, riding the galloping train like it was a bucking bronco.

"You might as well sit down," the man said over Dal's head to Mr. Sabatini. "I'll be out of here in two seconds. Then the table will be all yours."

Dal didn't want to, but his stepfather staggered over and plopped down in one of the upholstered chairs. "Thanks," he said, showing all his teeth in a grin. "Bit crowded today."

So Dal, who wasn't all that hungry, had to sit down, too.

"Eisenhauer," the man said, shaking hands with Mr. Sabatini. "H-A-U-E-R. No relation to the President. But I voted for him and will gladly do so again."

Dal pricked up his ears. Dwight David Eisenhower—H-O-W-E-R—also known as Ike, had been supreme commander in Europe during World War II. That's when Dal's real father, John Dallas Wilkins, Sr., had been killed in action—in Sicily, in 1943, when Dal was only two.

Ike had run for President of the United States the previous fall. Mr. Sabatini was a Democrat like Dal's mom, but he liked Ike because he had been in the war, too. He got grumpy whenever Dal's mom said Ike was a nice man, but . . .

"But what?" Mr. Sabatini wanted to know.

"But not too swift," said his mom, tapping her temple.

Mr. Sabatini and Dal's mom loved each other, but they sure didn't agree about politics. Dal's mom was for Adlai Stevenson, who had a hole in his shoe, because he was going to end all war once and for all.

At first Dal couldn't make up his mind who to vote for. They had pretend elections at school. One day Mr. Sabatini said, "Come on, I'll take you downtown to see Ike in person."

Dal didn't feel like it, but his mom gave him a push: "Do you good to get out of the house."

They went on a city bus with Mr. Sabatini's friend Mr. Lamberis. The men talked the whole way about Communism and the atom bomb. All either of them said to Dal was, "You having a good time?" When they got off, there were people as far as the eye could see. Mr. Sabatini boosted Dal up so he could sit on the statue of Cadillac, the founder of Detroit, and gaze out over everybody's head. Ike had a long coat on because it was f-freezing out. It was so cold it chilled your bones, Mr. Sabatini said, clapping his gloved hands to keep them warm. When the people cheered, Ike waved his hat. He sure looked like the President. Some other men got up and made speeches, too, but their words were scattered in the cold air.

Dal kept his eyes on Ike. He wondered if he had ever met his father during the war and, if so, whether he would recognize Dal up there on Cadillac's lap. Everyone said he was the spitting image of his late dad.

When the rally was over, the crowd surged together and lifted Dal off his feet. At first it was fun, but then so many coats pressed against his face he had trouble breathing. He didn't see either Mr. Sabatini or Mr. Lamberis. Then a gloved hand reached out of the crowd. Dal had never touched Mr. Sabatini's hand before, but he grabbed it, and the three of them pushed their way past Crowley's Department Store. As they were walking down a more or less empty street, Ike's limousine turned the corner and came slowly toward them. It was a black Cadillac convertible. Ike stared hard at Dal for about two seconds: *Eisenhower one, Eisenhower two.* Then he grinned and waved.

After that, Dal wore his I LIKE IKE button everywhere he went. He put an EISENHOWER/NIXON sticker down the back fender of his bike. His mom said, "Exactly. He appeals to eleven-year-old boys."

"Now, Helen . . ." Mr. Sabatini began.

Dal didn't care. Maybe someday *he* would be President—President John Dallas Wilkins, Jr.—only he would tell people to just call him Dal. He would take off his hat and wave it at the crowd. That was still a secret, though. Whenever anyone asked him, he said he was going out West to be a cowboy.

Mr. Eisenhauer—the man on the train—asked what their names were. Don't tell him, Dal thought as hard as he could, but it was impossible to get through to Mr. Sabatini with mental telepathy. His real name was Hercules Sabatini, but he always told people to call him Harry. Personally Dal would rather be Hercules than Harry any day.

"And this is my wife's son, Dal."

Dal waited to see what would happen. Sometimes when he was introduced, people said, "Dal! Where'd you ever get a name like that?" He liked his name because when his mom said Dal, he was who she meant. Plus, it was the name his friends knew him by. But he had to admit that if you said it over and over, "Dal, Dal, Dal, Dal, Dal," it didn't sound like a name. It didn't even sound like a word that meant anything.

Mr. Eisenhauer didn't even look at Dal. He just kept smearing stinky cheese on little bits of roll and sticking them into his gobber. (If "gobber" isn't a word, it should be.) He said, "You folks traveling for business or pleasure?"

"A bit of both," said Mr. Sabatini, waving to attract the waiter's attention. "We're on our way out to Idaho. I'm a crop inspector for Purity Seeds. The boy's coming along to give me a hand."

Dal kept his eyes on Mr. Eisenhauer. He didn't like him, but he didn't know why. Usually he hated a person's guts, then tried to figure out the reason. Mr. Eisenhauer acted nice. He had let them sit down at his table. But he was a liar. He said he was getting up in two seconds—*stinky cheese one, stinky cheese two*—and by now at least a million seconds had gone by.

Also, he smiled the whole time, but his smile was fake. Dal hoped that Mr. Sabatini could tell his smile was fake. The trouble with Mr. Sabatini was he thought that just about everybody was a nice guy, and not everybody was. When Dal had tried to explain this fact to him once, Mr. Sabatini just shook his head. "Now you're starting to sound like your mother," he said.

Dal knew he should act grown-up about his mom's getting married again, since *she* liked Mr. Sabatini, but he couldn't get used to having him and his daughter, Kate, live in their house with them.

Why couldn't Dal and his mom just go on the way they always had, with the Sabatinis down the street? Suddenly the house was too small. The bathroom was crowded with extra toothbrushes, a chipped water glass, Mr. Sabatini's shaving kit spread all over the place, not to mention his economy-size bottle of Wildroot Cream Oil. All the chairs downstairs had Kate's dolls in them: you had to look before you sat. He couldn't just go into his mom's bedroom anymore: Mr. Sabatini might be in there, stretched out on the bed in his suspenders and smelly socks. Plus, Dal never knew what he should call him. He couldn't say Dad because he wasn't his real dad; he'd feel weird saying Harry. Most of the time he didn't call him anything, though in his mind he still called him Mr. Sabatini, because that was the name he had always known him by.

Dal ordered a chicken sandwich for lunch, but when it came, it had green gunk on it. Mr. Sabatini said the green gunk was "delicious" watercress mayonnaise. "Don't be so finicky. Try at least one bite."

Dal looked at the sandwich and felt tired. He *was* a finicky eater, he knew that, but why would anyone want to wreck a perfectly good chicken sandwich? With both men watching, he forced himself to touch the green gunk with his tongue and almost felt like throwing up. His stepfather shook his head apologetically at Mr. Eisenhauer, picked up the sandwich in both hands, and took a bite out of it. Mr. Sabatini would eat just about anything.

The waiter came back, and this time Dal ordered a grilled cheese sandwich. The good thing about a grilled cheese sandwich is that at least you know what you're getting.

Mr. Sabatini and Mr. Eisenhauer were yakking away like they had known each other for years, instead of only for about twenty minutes. Why did grown-ups like to talk so much, and why did they always talk about boring things like life insurance? Luckily Dal was sitting by the window. He squinted through the rainy light at the fields rushing by. Detroit was a city; this was the country. He had tried to explain the difference to his stepsister, Kate, when they all went to Holland, Michigan, last Easter for their family honeymoon. Mr. Sabatini drove, and Dal's mom sat in front where Dal usually sat. Dal had to sit in the back with Kate. He tried to act like a big brother. He gave Kate a test. "Is where we are now country or city?"

Kate stuck her tongue out the side of her mouth and said, "City?" Kate was five. With little kids it was hopeless.

Kate had wanted to come on *this* trip, too, but Mr. Sabatini said, "Help me here, Helen," and his mom quickly said, "Now we've talked about this, Kate. Your dad and Dal need some time by themselves, to get to know each other. *I* need someone to stay with me." Kate lay on the living floor, kicking the carpet with her heels and screaming that no one loved her. The tears ran down her temples and into her hair.

Dal got down on the floor next to her. "I'll bring you something back from Idaho, Kate," he said.

"What?" she asked suspiciously, her heels suspended in midair.

"I can't tell you or it won't be a surprise. But it will be something"—he held his arms wide—"g-g-r-rreat."

Really, though, Dal was of two minds about the trip. He wanted to go out West, and he didn't even mind if Mr. Sabatini came along. He just wished his mom was going, too, so he'd have someone to talk to and wouldn't have to be alone all the time with practically a stranger. He secretly knew that Mr. Sabatini felt the same way. One night when he couldn't fall asleep, Dal had sat at the top of the stairs and overheard Mr. Sabatini say, "What am I supposed to talk to him about for two and a half months? He's a good kid and everything. It's just that we live on different planets."

But when the time came and he got to leave school a whole week early, Dal felt important. He knew all the other kids would be watching through the tall windows as he followed his stepfather out into sunshine and freedom. (If you want to know the truth, he felt like someone who might grow up to be President someday.)

Kate and his mom had come to the station in Detroit to see them off. Dal was having cold feet, but he didn't want his mom to know because she would worry, so he kept smiling like an idiot. He didn't even try to turn his face away when his mom licked her handkerchief and smoothed the front of his hair back—he hated it when she did that. When the conductor came along, crying, "All aboard!" Mr. Sabatini shouted, "Kate!" Kate jumped. She had been talking to her new Raggedy Ann. When Kate heard her name, she grabbed the doll by one arm and started after him. "No, Kate!" Mr. Sabatini said from the stairs of the railway car. "Go with Mommy." (Kate already called Dal's mom Mommy.) Dal watched the whole thing. Kate was too little to understand what was going on, but he wasn't. He followed Mr. Sabatini's back into the railway car, feeling like he was on his own now.

If Kate had come along, Dal would have been stuck with her, but at least he could have made the *oink, oink* sound. Kate would have put her napkin over her face and cracked up. He wished there was at least one other kid on the train. If you're the only kid, after a while you start feeling invisible. (If you were really invisible, you could go anywhere you wanted, right up Kay St. John's front steps and into her house. He made up a story about it.)

Mr. Eisenhauer kept asking Mr. Sabatini personal questions like how much money he made. "I don't like to talk about it, Harry," he said (so why did he then?), "but my brother-in-law went in an automobile accident when he was about your age." He leaned forward and said in a loud whisper, "Decapitated," glancing for a billionth of a second at Dal. "Only, thank God," he added in his regular voice, "his policy was paid up. I saw to that. Now his little family is doing fine."

What was that? *Decapitated?* Dal wanted to ask Mr. Sabatini what it meant, but not while Mr. Eisenhauer was there. He kept saying the word over and over in his head, so he wouldn't forget it. It probably meant squished.

Dal wished Mr. Sabatini would tell Mr. Eisenhauer something *he* knew. He knew all about flowers and vegetables. That's how he and his mom had met. Mr. Sabatini was always helping her with her garden. Dal knew the batting averages for all the players on the Detroit Tigers but probably wouldn't get a chance to say them.

Mr. Eisenhauer was a know-it-all, but *judge not that ye be not judged.*

Dal was so bored he felt like reading. His books were packed in one of the suitcases. Besides, he didn't really feel like reading; that's just how bored he was.

When Mr. Eisenhauer finally got off the train in a town called Gary, he seemed very pleased with himself. "I'll be in touch," he said, waving.

Dal and Mr. Sabatini went to the club car to wet their whistles. They didn't have Squirt, so Dal got Canada Dry. He always wondered why they called it Canada Dry and not Canada Wet.

"Are you going to buy insurance from him?" he asked when they had found a couple of empty seats together.

"I don't know," said Mr. Sabatini, lighting one of his smelly cigarillos. "I probably *should* take out a policy on my life. For Helen and you kids. You never know. Course I'd have to pass the physical, but I don't think there'd be any problem there, do you?"

He took off his suit jacket and rolled up his sleeve. He was a short man, but when he made a muscle, a little hill popped up in the crook of his arm.

"Go ahead, feel it," he said, blowing smoke the other way.

Dal felt his biceps with his thumb and index finger. It sure was hard.

"Now you make a muscle," Mr. Sabatini said with his cigarillo between his teeth. "Go on."

Dal sighed. He knew he was too skinny. He squeezed as hard as he could. His whole arm was shaking. Mr. Sabatini felt Dal's arm in a couple of places, his face turned sideways like he was a doctor. At least he didn't make any comments.

Dal had assumed that the train would go on forever. So far they had traveled through southern Michigan and a tiny piece of Indiana and had just crossed into Illinois. But at Union Station, Chicago, the train stopped, and everybody got out. Dal followed his stepfather through a sort of underground tunnel. Mr. Sabatini briefly set their suitcases on the floor—a small island in a river of people, mostly men in business suits and hats, hurrying every which way. The ticket he took from his suit pocket dangled from his chin to his chest. (Dal was traveling half fare; *his* ticket was just a piece of paper with writing on it, stapled to the back of his stepfather's.) Mr. Sabatini looked at the ticket, then squinted at the numbers painted on the walls.

"Come on!" he shouted. "No time to lose!" Grabbing up most of their luggage, he sprinted ahead.

Dal's bedroll kept coming undone. He had been twisting the drawstring, trying to stuff some of the material under it. When Mr. Sabatini took off, Dal hiked the bedroll up into his armpit, picked up his straw-colored suitcase, and ran after him. It was all he could do to keep Mr. Sabatini in sight. They ran like that—Mr. Sabatini twenty feet in front, calling over his shoulder, "Come on, Dal," Dal running so hard he had a stitch in his side—through the tiled tunnels and down a metal staircase marked TO TRACK NUMBER 9.

CHAPTER 2

THE PULLMAN

Their train was waiting at the platform. As soon as they climbed aboard, heaving their luggage up ahead of them, they were in another world. Hush. People were talking in low voices, glancing at one another and smiling, calmly organizing their belongings. It was like they were all members of a secret club. Dal stood catching his breath. He remembered now Mr. Sabatini saying that in Chicago they would catch their real train, a Pullman, which would take them out West. The porter said his name was Emory. He insisted on carrying all their luggage: three suitcases and two bedrolls. Halfway down the corridor he stopped at a pair of facing seats and examined a piece of paper pinned to one of them. It said "Mr. Sabatini and Son." (It should have said "and Stepson.")

"Here you go, gentlemen," said Emory, stacking their luggage on one of the seats.

All up and down the car the seats like these were being converted into berths, an upper and a lower. The lady across the aisle said something to Mr. Sabatini. She had two little kids who leaned out from behind her to look at Dal, then quickly leaned back again.

A man in a white uniform came by with a xylophone to announce the first sitting for supper. "That's us," Mr. Sabatini said, wiping his face with his handkerchief.

Emory said, "Y'all go eat your suppers now. I'll get your bed ready for you."

* * *

Everything in the dining car was fancy. The table had a stiff white cloth and goblets with water and tinkly ice cubes. The plates, with a picture of the train on them, were framed by a heavy knife and two forks and another knife and spoon at the top. Just as they were getting comfortable, the train started to move. A little jerk, and then they were in motion. Slowly, steadily, they glided out of the tunnel into the crisscross of train tracks that was Union Station, out into the purple evening. Chicago was all around them, bright with neon signs. The rain had stopped. They rode through train yards, across a metal bridge with pale blue water underneath. The train gathered speed and tooted its whistle.

Meanwhile, inside, they all pretended they weren't on a moving train. Glasses tinkled, the couple at the next table giggled, the waiter brought bowls of cold consommé, and Dal sighed a huge sigh. This was more fun than anything he had ever done. In the privacy of his mind, he was telling his friend Jimmy Beard about it. How the silverware was so heavy it stayed put, even when the train went flying around a corner. How his stepfather let him order anything his "heart desired"—"Let's put some meat on them bones." So Dal had ordered fried chicken and mashed potatoes and peas, and they had come with all the dry, warm rolls and butter you could eat. He eyed the gravy suspiciously, but everything turned out to be lump-free and yummy. (Except that he wasn't sure about the mushrooms and put them carefully to one side. What if by mistake someone had put in a toadstool?) Mr. Sabatini ordered filet mignon, which is a piece of steak the size of a hamburger (a gyp). "It's the best part of the cow," he said with his mouth full. "Want a bite?"

"No, thank you," said Dal politely. (The inside was red.)

Sometimes when you ordered milk in a restaurant, it came lukewarm and tasted funny, but the milk on the Pullman was freezing cold and delicious.

Mr. Sabatini started talking to the people at the next-door table. Dal kept himself occupied by looking out the window. If he cupped his hands to the glass, he could already see darkening fields—Chicago was long gone—but if he sat back, he saw the inside of the dining car and a man built like a small refrigerator sitting next to a skinny boy. The boy's breath fogged up the window, and when his forehead touched the glass, it left a smudge.

For dessert Dal had vanilla ice cream in a pewter dish. It was so cold it had small pieces of ice in it.

To get back to their seats, they had to walk through four enemy cars. Dal wondered what would happen if you ran against the direction of the train. Would you go slower because the train was speeding the other way? Or what if you ran *with* the train? Would you lope like a wild antelope, running faster than you ever had before? He thought about asking, but it was probably a question that everyone else knew the answer to, and he didn't want Mr. Sabatini to think he was an ignoramus. One of the cars they passed through was some kind of service car without seats. Tomorrow Dal would come back there and conduct some experiments.

Back in their car they found that their seats had been turned into beds, an upper and lower berth. Theirs was on top. Already the lights had been dimmed. People in the aisles smiled shyly as they got ready for bed. A woman in curlers brushed past; she wore a bathrobe and carried her toothbrush and tooth powder in front of her. A pair of hairy legs dangled from one of the upper berths; there were slippers on the feet. Dal had seen a girl his age in one of the other cars. She saw him, too, but pretended she hadn't. If he walked back—he could always say he had left his new watch in the dining car—would he catch a glimpse of her getting into her pajamas? It was something to think about.

When the bathroom was free, he and Mr. Sabatini both went in. If you were a man and boy, you could go in together, but Dal still felt funny. He wished Mr. Sabatini would at least turn the other way and not make comments on his aim. The bathroom was tiny. Dal managed to put on his official Detroit Tigers pajamas, standing first on one shoe and then the other, without once touching the damp floor with his bare feet. The sign said DO NOT FLUSH WHILE TRAIN IS STANDING IN THE STATION, but since the train was moving through the countryside, it was all right to now. Moving, nothing: it was whipping along so fast that the windows panted for air. Every now and then, as they approached a level crossing, the frantic *ding, ding, ding, ding* of the warning bells was answered by the train's *waa-a-waaaaaho.* They were in something great, huge, wild, impatient, unstoppable, growling through the night like *Tyrannosaurus rex,* and meanwhile, the liquid in the toilet bowl swirled lazily and disappeared with a gulp through a hole—right onto the tracks! Where else could it go? P-U.

Dal's heart was thumping as he climbed into their berth. It had dawned on him that he and Mr. Sabatini would be sharing the same bed. Dal had never slept with a grown-up before, besides his mom. What if he had a bad dream? What if he had to go in the middle of the night?

Mr. Sabatini held up an unlit cigarillo. "The time it takes to smoke that and I'll be back. You okay?"

Dal nodded. As soon as his stepfather was gone, he explored the berth. It had its own little light and a basket shelf to put things in and a looped plastic strap to hold on to in case their train crashed into one coming the other way. After a while he lay on his back, letting the train rock him. He hadn't meant to fall asleep—and he woke with a start when Mr. Sabatini's voice whispered, "Good night," to someone. The bed sagged once as he climbed in beside Dal, taking up most of the room. After trying several positions, Mr. Sabatini curled up with his back to Dal. He smelled like a cigarillo and— *sniff, sniff*—something sweet besides: Wildroot Cream Oil, the tonic he used to slick his hair down with.

Mr. Sabatini looked back over his shoulder, and Dal froze. He was afraid Mr. Sabatini had caught him making his bunny nose. But all he said was, "Ain't nothing like sleeping on a Pullman." Then he put his head back down on the little pillow they gave you and started snoring like a buffalo.

Why did he say "ain't" when he knew better? Because it made what he said sound true, true, true, that's why.

Dal stared at the back of Mr. Sabatini's neck. It was covered with black hair. (No wonder he was "Harry.") After a while Dal turned over. Carefully lifting the shade away from the edge of the window, he peeked out.

Field after field rushed by, and every once in a while a dark, lonely-looking house appeared and disappeared in the moonlight. No matter how fast the train rattled along in its tracks, the moon, an almost perfect half circle, stayed in the same place in the sky. Dal stared at its quiet light, as if hypnotized. He wondered if his father—his *real* father—was up there somewhere and, if so, whether he could see Dal's face looking out.

Would he be proud of him for taking this trip all by himself?

Dal didn't really remember his dad, except for one moment that was like looking through the wrong end of a pair of binoculars. It was snowing out, there were Christmas lights on in all the stores, and a man in a uniform carried him in his arms with a lot of packages. When the man laughed, you could see his breath. Only maybe it wasn't a real memory. Maybe it was something someone had told him about.

Dal dropped the shade back into place. He lay as close to the window as he could, trying to make his body into a straight line.

A border of bright sunshine framed the window. Beyond the heavy curtain on the aisle side of their berth, people were talking. That meant a new day had begun, the longest in Dal's life (so far). He (1) ate breakfast while Mr. Sabatini read the newspaper. After a while he said, "Can I have the comics?" Mr. Sabatini sighed, like it was a lot of trouble, but handed them over without a word.

(2) Walked past the girl his age. All the berths had been transformed into ordinary-looking pairs of seats, facing each other. She sat alone, reading a book. She wore a white blouse and a plaid skirt and penny loafers with pennies stuck in the slots. Her hair had been neatly brushed so that the ends curled up into the sunshine. He stared at her, but she didn't look up—she just turned the page and kept on reading. Stuck up, he thought disgustedly, trying to see the title. In the course of the day he walked past her thirteen times.

(3) Sat in his seat and looked out the window. They were really out West now, no people for miles around. Lots of scenery, though.

(4) Made up stories about the girl his age. *And the next time he went past, she looked up. He said, "Hi, you want to help me do some experiments?" "Okay," she said, clapping her book shut. When she jumped up, her skirt bounced away from her knees.* His story made him sad and tired. Nobody in his right mind went up to a complete stranger and asked her if she wanted to help him with his experiments. The most he could hope for was that they might meet by accident. *He was running down the corridor, unable to stop; she was coming through the door—*

"Dal."

"Huh?"

"Don't just sit there all day, staring out the window. Get up and stretch your legs."

(5) Drank twenty-two paper cones full of water. You could taste the paper.

(6) Went to the bathroom eleven times.

(7) Knelt on the seat to open his straw-colored suitcase. He had inherited the suitcase from his aunt Betty, who had died of old age. It had come with a hairbrush in it, which Dal threw away, and it smelled like an attic but was otherwise okay. (There were secret side pockets you could put things in.) Dal had packed it himself and was the only one who knew what was inside.

He took out the book his mom had given him for the trip and quickly shut the lid. Maybe the girl his age would walk through their car and notice him reading.

Excuse me, what's the title of your book?

He looked. *Little Britches,* by Ralph Moody. He read the first page. Sometimes when he read a book, it was like being at the movies and he could see everything that was going on. But to make that happen, first he had to blot out everything else around him. He had to read every word and every sentence, making his eyes move from left to right. If he stopped concentrating for even a second or if his eyes got tired and gradually crossed, the story disappeared, and he was left staring at the shapes of paragraphs or at the spaces between words angling down the page. The book was all right. It was about a boy who went out West with his family.

Mr. Sabatini leaned across the aisle and said in his too-loud voice, "My stepson, the bookworm. He gets that from his mother." Dal read one more sentence, quietly shut the book, and put it back in the suitcase. He didn't feel that much like reading anyway. He wondered if the girl his age still had her nose in her book. Kay St. John was always reading, too. Why did girls like to read so much?

(8) Entertained the two little kids in the next seats so that Mr. Sabatini and their mother could get up and stretch their legs. ("Sure you don't mind?" she said. "Uh-uh.") Dal was getting good at making up games, but little kids on trains are squirmy and sweaty. They kept wriggling up next to him. When their mom finally did come back, alone, he played with them a little while longer. Then he heard himself say, "I have a headache." She was leafing through the *Saturday Evening Post.* She had on bright red lipstick.

"Come back and play with your puzzle," she said to her kids, winking at him. "Dal needs some time out."

(9) Went exploring (and to look for Mr. Sabatini). Got hollered at for tapping the seats as he passed. A man's head popped up. "Do you mind?" So he just pretended to tap.

(10) Did some experiments in the car without seats, running with the train and running against it. Nobody came through the door.

(11) Watched the waiters set the tables for lunch. Finally one of them said, "The diner is closed until lunchtime"—i.e., scram.

(12) Flopped down next to Mr. Sabatini, who was sitting in their seat, reading the *Reader's Digest.* He felt like saying, "Where were you?" Instead he just folded his arms and sighed loudly. Mr. Sabatini looked at him. "Something the matter?"

"No," said Dal, the liar.

(13) Ate lunch and looked at the scenery some more. (Mountains.)

(14) Got off the train with Mr. Sabatini, late in the afternoon, in Laramie, Wyoming, to stretch their legs. It was cold outside. The whistle blew. They quickly got back on again.

F i n a l l y evening came. The next stop was Pocatello, Idaho. Dal and his stepfather stood by one of the doors, their suitcases all lined up. Emory was joking with Mr. Sabatini. When the train stopped, he handed down their suitcases and followed the last one onto the platform. When Mr. Sabatini gave him some money—Dal couldn't see how much—Emory said, "*Thank* you, sir. *Thank* you."

While the train stood in the station, Dal counted the cars: seventeen. As they were walking along the platform, the train started to move again. For three whole seconds—*decapitated one, decapitated two, decapitated three*—they and the train were going at the same speed. The girl his age stood at the window. She stared at him, and he stared at her. He didn't know her name or where she was going; he would probably never see her again. The train picked up speed, the brightly lit cars hurrying each other into the night. The little kids waved from their window. Their mother loomed behind them. She was smoking a cigarette and looking at something over his head. The iron wheels found the right rhythm on the tracks. It was like a tune in your head—*roola, roola, rack; roola, roola, rack.* Pretty soon the noise vanished into thin air. All you could see was the end of the train, cabooseless, a door that led nowhere, getting smaller.

With the train gone, the world seemed very still. Somewhere a dog barked. Dal's idea of the West came mostly from TV shows: *Hopalong Cassidy* and *The Lone Ranger*. He didn't really expect there to be cowboys with six-shooters hanging around the station, but he wouldn't have minded a friendly Indian or two. The air was sweet with a smell he had never smelled before. He meant to ask what it was, but Mr. Sabatini had collected their suitcases and was already headed toward the station. Dal hugged his bedroll in one arm, gripped his straw-colored suitcase, and stumbled after him on ground that didn't move.

CHAPTER 3

THE GREEN
PICKUP TRUCK

After breakfast the next morning they jaywalked to the shady side of the street, where Mr. Sabatini jumped on the running board of a green pickup truck. "Like it?" he said. Before Dal could answer, he added, "You better. It's our only transportation for the summer."

Dal walked around the truck and examined it from every angle. It had big scooped-out wheel guards like an old lady's skirts. The roof of the cab was a different green from the rest of the truck, as if its bulging head had baked in the sun too long. The bottom half—the wheels, the sides, the tailgate—looked like they had been dipped in dirt. Dal climbed in on the passenger's side. There was a gash in the middle of the seat that someone had tried to tape shut. Some stuffing seeped out. If he sat all the way back, his feet didn't quite touch the floor. On the dashboard there was a built-in clock and a radio with a chrome speaker. The cab smelled of sweat and dust.

"Well?" said Mr. Sabatini, looking up from the Standard Oil map he had spread out on the hood.

Dal jumped to the sidewalk and clapped his hands clean. "It's neat," he said.

His stepfather showed him the route they would be taking— mostly Route 30, through towns with names like American Falls, Heyburn, Burley—finally to Eden, a dot half hidden in the fold. Just seeing the name of the town they been traveling two days to get to made something happen to Dal's insides. He was a bottle of pop whose top somebody had just flipped: he could feel the bubbles rising. Mr. Sabatini was in a good mood, too, whistling as they carried their suitcases across the street from the hotel. He climbed in back to make sure everything was wedged in tight.

"Better get the lead out," he said cheerfully.

On the way to Eden Dal saw his first rattlesnake. They were in real cowboy country now, flatlands as far as the eye could see, with nothing growing except for mesquite and sagebrush. Sagebrush: that's what Mr. Sabatini said flavored the air with its sweet, dry smell. An occasional tumbleweed raced them down the highway or blew across the road in front of them. Not many cars passed in either direction. As usual Mr. Sabatini didn't say much to him, but Dal was getting used to just sitting next to him, thinking his own thoughts.

Mr. Sabatini pulled onto the shoulder and stopped the truck. Dal looked at him; they were in the middle of nowhere. "Have to see a man about a dog," Mr. Sabatini said, swinging open his door and dropping to the ground. "I have to see a man about a dog" means you have to take a leak. Imagine if there really was a man with a dog, and that's what you did.

Dal got out, too. He stood about twenty feet away from Mr. Sabatini, facing the other way. And that's when he saw it: a baby rattler, sleekly coiled back and forth on itself, flicking its black tongue. Its rattle shook like crazy, filling the air with a dry electric sound. Dal's heart was pounding, but he was more curious than afraid.

"There's a snake," he said in his regular voice.

Mr. Sabatini came running. In two seconds he stood between Dal and the rattler, holding out his short arms like a safety patrol boy. "The little ones are just as dangerous as the big ones," he said, walking Dal back.

"I know that," Dal said, trying to see around him.

Standing side by side, they peed in the desert, keeping an eye out for other snakes. The arc Mr. Sabatini made was twice as long as his, Dal couldn't help noticing out of the corner of his eye. He tilted up, but it didn't help.

Then, over the rainbow, Dal saw something he could hardly believe: GOLD! Embedded in rocks, it shone like nuts in a candy bar.

"Look," he said, quickly putting himself back together and kneeling among the rocks. Gold everywhere, bright, shining nuggets the size of his thumb! *We're rich!* he thought, gathering up as many rocks as he could hold. There had to be thousands of dollars' worth, maybe millions. When they got to the motel, he would call home. "Hey, Mom, guess what?"

Mr. Sabatini finished more leisurely, rubbed his hands with dirt, and slapped them on the sides of his khaki pants. "What you got there?" he said, taking the piece Dal handed him and holding it up to the sky.

"Did you think this was gold?" he asked, throwing the rock in the air and catching it. He grinned at Dal, then laughed. "Ha-ha," he said, throwing back his bullet-shaped head. "Ha-ha-ha!" He put his hands on his thighs and squatted down to laugh better. "I'm sorry, Dal, but you should have seen the look on your face."

Dal looked at him as though he had gone crazy.

"It's mica," Mr. Sabatini said, still grinning. He tossed the rock back to Dal. "They're talking about using it to make windows in rocket ships. It's very durable, and see, it flakes off in sheets." He held a tiny flake up to his eye like a monocle. "You can almost see through it."

Dal stared around blankly. "But there's a whole lot of it," he said desperately. "We could empty our suitcases. We could—"

"Whoa," said Mr. Sabatini, holding up both hands. "Keep in mind, anything we put in our suitcases, we have to lug back with us in August. Hey, I know. Why don't you grab a few pieces for your rock collection?"

Dal got to his feet. For a shining moment he had felt rich; now he felt dirt poor. "I don't have a rock collection," he mumbled, looking at his gym shoes. He hated Mr. Sabatini for laughing at him like that. Jerk, he said in his mind. Never tell you anything again.

"You have the Petoskey stones I gave you," Mr. Sabatini said. "And the rose quartz you found on our honeymoon. I bet we'll find lots of rocks out here we don't have in Michigan."

"That's all right," Dal said, emptying his pockets. But when Mr. Sabatini said, "Well, better hit the road," Dal shouted, "Wait!" and picked up the two best pieces.

When they were back in the truck and Mr. Sabatini had started the engine again, he looked at Dal and sighed. "Be nice to strike it rich, eh? Buy your mom a washing machine. New bikes for you and Kate." Dal let his feet drop against the front of his seat but didn't say anything. His bike at home worked all right, but it was old and junky. He had painted it silver, but it didn't come out the way he expected. If they had really found gold, they could have bought a TV so he wouldn't have to go over to Jimmy Beard's when he wanted to watch *The Lone Ranger*.

Mr. Sabatini looked at him again. "Scoot over. I want to show you something."

"That's all right," Dal said.

"Come on. Don't be a spoilsport."

Sighing, Dal wriggled to the middle of the seat. Mr. Sabatini guided his hand to the knob at the top of the shifter.

"This is first," he said, driving along the side of the road. "Hear it? *Vroom, vroom?* That means we have to shift to second, up here." No cars were coming. They pulled out onto the highway and went into third. Pretty soon they were doing 65 mph. His stepfather kept glancing at him, instead of watching the road. "Think you can remember that? Someday you're going to need to know how to drive a car. In my opinion a boy can't start too early."

Dal scooted back over to his side of the truck. "Thanks," he muttered.

They drove into Eden, Idaho (population 427), just as the sun was going down. It was the smallest town Dal had ever seen. He had fallen asleep during the long ride, but was wide-awake now, sitting forward with one hand on the dash. On the left, as you entered town, there was a gas station with its Flying Red Horse sign against the pink sunset. Then came five blocks of lit-up stores, including a movie theater with a bright marquee. Down every side street for two blocks stood small, glimmering houses; beyond lay farmland and the evening sky. While he'd been napping, they had driven out of the desert and into this lush valley, watered, Mr. Sabatini said, by the Snake River. Main Street, Eden, was the same road they had been on all day, only now they were doing 30 mph instead of 65. At the far edge of town the road turned back into a highway and disappeared through trees downhill.

The last store on the left was a combination grocery store and a Honk-and-We'll-Come-Out-and-Fill-It gas station. A small sign said WE GIVE GREEN STAMPS. They parked the pickup in the deepening shade, behind a tractor, got out, and slammed their doors. They stood for a second in the cooling air, while Mr. Sabatini looked at Dal. "Remember," he said, "stand up straight, shoulders back. Like this." He put his own shoulders back as far as they would go and puffed out his chest like an eagle.

Dal stood as straight as he could. Following his stepfather into the store, he felt like a walking ladder.

Inside, the store smelled nice. The air was cool. "Well, lookee who's here," said the man behind the counter, carefully hooking the sidepieces of his glasses around each ear. "Back for another summer?" he asked, shaking hands with Mr. Sabatini.

"Yes, and you'll never guess what I've been up to. I got myself hitched again, to the prettiest woman in Detroit."

Dal looked at his stepfather. He had never heard him talk about his mom before. He thought she was pretty, too, but then she was his mother.

"Oh, and I got a stepson into the bargain."

The man reached across the counter and shook Dal's hand.

A woman came out of the back, wiping her hands on the front of her apron. She smiled at Dal even before he was introduced and shook hands, too. Their name was Turner. (Why did people shake hands? Dogs sniffed each other. Not that he would want to sniff the Turners.)

Dal couldn't help feeling proud. Here they had traveled nearly two thousand miles by Pullman and pickup, walked into the first store they came to, and the people there knew them and acted like they were glad to see them.

Mr. Sabatini was all smiles. He whistled under his breath as he pushed his cart around the store. Dal imitated him. In a voice anybody could hear, he said, "What should I get?"

"Whatever you think we'll need. Mrs. Turner, slice me a pound of that good American cheese."

Dal's mom always had a list when she went shopping, and you got a treat only if you *didn't* bug her for one. But his stepfather let him get anything he wanted. He held up a bag of potato chips; Mr. Sabatini said, "Throw 'em in!" He was busy piling items up on the counter so that Mrs. Turner could ring them up and pack them neatly into two cardboard boxes. "Ice cream!" his stepfather said, giving Dal a push toward the giant freezer, the kind you lifted the lid of. "Pick the flavor you like best."

As Mr. Sabatini paid, Mrs. Turner counted out nearly half a sheet of Green Stamps. "Here," she said, handing them to Dal along with an empty book to put them in. "I reckon you'll want these. You can earn good merchandise."

Back in the truck Mr. Sabatini stuck out his hand. "Harry Sabatini. Put it there." Dal just looked at him. "I think we need a little lesson in shaking hands," his stepfather said.

Oh, brother, Dal thought, but he reached over and let Mr. Sabatini shake his hand. "Dal Wilkins," he said politely. "Pleased to meet you."

"Harder!" said Mr. Sabatini.

Dal gripped his hand harder. His stepfather's hand may have been small, but it was stronger than an eagle's claw.

"Harder! Try to hurt me!"

Dal scrunched his face up and squeezed with all his might.

Mr. Sabatini laughed. "That's the ticket," he said, letting go. "Shake hands like that, and people will know you mean business."

CHAPTER 4

THE GARDEN
OF EDEN MOTEL

Now that the long trip was coming to an end, Dal wished it could last a little bit longer. Mr. Sabatini must have felt the same way because he drove back through town slowly, turning right at the sign of the Flying Red Horse and right again into the courtyard of the GARDEN OF EDEN MOTEL. Some of the lights in the big oval had burned out, but a bright strip of pink neon underneath said VACANCY. Not a lot of other people seemed to be staying at the Garden of Eden that evening. Only two units had cars parked in front, a beat-up '47 Hudson and a brand-new Ford from Texas. Dal had never seen a Texas license plate before and went over to look at it.

In the center of the courtyard was an empty swimming pool, dandelions growing in the cracks of the cement bottom. Some of the numbers on the doors to people's rooms were missing, only you could still see the ghosts of the numbers in the paint. Dal and his stepfather stood still for a few seconds, the way you do when you finally reach your destination, watching the clouds travel on overhead. In the shadows a cat scurried so fast it looked like it had twelve legs. Dal's stepfather cupped his hands over his mouth and called out, "Hello, Mrs. Pucket!" To Dal he said, "She's a little hard-of-hearing."

The motel was two buildings, two sides of a square. A walkway led around the side to a pretty house, painted white with dark green shutters and surrounded by a white picket fence. A sign on the gate said OFFICE. Once inside the gate, they were in a well-tended garden with fruit trees reaching to the second floor. "Apricots," said his stepfather, holding down a branch so that Dal could see the fuzzy green fruit. He rang the bell and knocked on the screen door, which banged against the frame. Finally, he leaned his head back and shouted up to a lighted window on the second floor, *"Miss-iz Puck-et!"*

Dal elbowed him because the shadow of an old lady had appeared behind the screen. She held up a small block of wood from which a key dangled. "Well, glory be," she said. "I've been expecting *you* since Friday night."

"No, no," said Mr. Sabatini. "I said we'd probably get here *last* night, but we got in a little late and spent the night in Pocatello. We're here now, though. This is my stepson I told you about on the phone."

Mrs. Pucket opened the screen door and came outside. "So you're the stepson? How do you do?" Dal wasn't sure how hard he should squeeze an old lady's hand, but she gripped his hand like she was trying to break his bones. She also peered at him close up. "I'll tell you one thing," she said. "His mama sure must be a pretty woman."

"She is," said Mr. Sabatini.

"Just look at them eyelashes. Why, a girl would be just thrilled to have eyelashes like that."

Oh, brother, Dal thought.

His stepfather said quickly, "Oh, he's a regular boy."

"You're a right nice-looking boy," Mrs. Pucket exclaimed. "Don't mind me. Your stepdaddy has been coming here for the last four years. I guess I know *him* pretty well."

"Three," said Mr. Sabatini mildly.

"He always stays in Unit Number 4. Come on. I'll show you. No sense standing around here all night." She led the way out of the garden, pausing to hold the gate open for them. Over her shoulder she said, "We've had it ready since Friday night. Turned away a couple of people who otherwise would have stayed."

Mr. Sabatini rolled his eyes, but then he took a couple of quick steps to keep up with her. "How's my buddy Len?"

"Len? Oh, you know, like sorrow, here today, gone tomorrow. He's moved back since the divorce, bless his heart. Be tickled pink to see you."

Unit Number 4, when they finally got the door open, smelled like nobody had stayed in it since the year before, but his stepfather went around opening the windows, and soon a slight breeze moved through the room.

While his stepfather and Mrs. Pucket blabbed, Dal went exploring. First he opened a door that was off to one side and stepped into the tiniest bedroom he had ever seen, most of it taken up with one square bed. Squeezed against the wall was a chest of drawers, and next to that were a wooden chair and a metal wastebasket that looked like somebody had kicked the side in. Stretched across the far corner was a warped wooden rod to hang your clothes on.

Dal sat down on the bed, which was soft and springy. It bounced up and down and sideways. His heart sank. If he had to share this bed with Mr. Sabatini, he'd end up on the floor. But when he went back into the main room, his stepfather interrupted himself to say, "That's where you're going to be."

"What about you?" Dal asked.

"I'm sleeping right here." He patted the davenport he was sitting on. It had a green skirt thingy that barely covered its wooden legs.

"That's not fair."

"It's where I slept last year, by choice. The bed's a little soft for a grown man."

Mrs. Pucket was rocking in the rocking chair, also green. She seemed pleased to have company. Probably she was lonely.

Dal went into the bathroom, which had all the fixtures you'd expect, but on a miniature scale. Next to the toilet was a sink barely big enough for one person to wash his face in, and crowded in the corner stood a narrow shower stall, the curtain patched with black tape. A stained water glass was perched on the narrow windowsill. Dal tried to rinse it with his finger. The water tasted funny, so he spit it out.

The kitchen was in the main room. A small electric stove stood in the far corner. Dal had never seen an electric stove before and couldn't wait to try it. A stoutish refrigerator, its door like a frozen overcoat, stood with its shoulders back against the wall. On shelves above the sink were plates and glasses and cups and saucers. In the table drawer were knives, forks, and spoons, plus assorted gadgets. And under the sink were pots and pans. Everywhere the yellowish linoleum had been worn through to the wood or was curling up at the edges.

Dal sighed a deep sigh. Unit Number 4 had everything a person could desire.

He plopped down on the davenport next to Mr. Sabatini. Mrs. Pucket was a nice lady, but she stayed about a million years. Dal heard her say, "I had a man come, but couldn't keep him, not at the wages they ask nowadays. There's too much work for a seventy-two-year-old woman with arthritis. I guess sooner or later I'll have to sell. Don't suppose you know of anyone who'd like to buy a motel? Good location. It's an opportunity for a young family with ambition."

Dal quickly looked at his stepfather—it would be neat to own a motel; they could fix up the pool, add a diving board—but Mr. Sabatini just stood up and said, "Better bring in the groceries," and Mrs. Pucket stood up, too, saying, "Where are my manners at? Here I am talking your ears off. If you need anything, holler."

They followed her outside, where darkness was settling over the courtyard. To Dal she said, "Come over and visit anytime. I like to see children playing in the garden. I keep cookies in the cookie jar, in case one of my grandkids comes to visit."

"He's going to meet one of your grandkids tomorrow night, at the Fosters'. I called Jerry from the station, and he said they were putting on a shindig for us, sort of a welcome picnic."

They watched her hurry home, her elbows and big hands and feet twinkling in the neon light. Then they carried in the groceries and their suitcases. The ice cream wouldn't fit in the freezing compartment because it was an igloo. Dal found an ice pick in the table drawer and began chipping away at the bulging ice. His stepfather meanwhile wiped the dead flies out of a pan and found a can opener in the table drawer.

Dal set the table for two, using toilet paper for napkins, then got down the dimestore china from the cupboard above the sink and counted out knives and forks from the table drawer. When the hash began to be crispy on the bottom, Mr. Sabatini turned it over with a pancake flipper and cracked four eggs on top of the mounds of chopped meat and potatoes. He covered the skillet with a metal lid that tilted to one side.

Dal eyed the corned beef hash and eggs suspiciously but didn't say anything. He was peeling carrots for their vegetable. While the corned beef hissed and spattered in the skillet, Mr. Sabatini boiled water for his coffee. Dal fetched the milk from the fridge. It came in a cardboard carton, not like back home, where the milkman delivered it in glass bottles. The label said "homogenized," but Dal shook it anyway, just to be on the safe side. He also put out the Wonder bread and a stick of butter and a jar of Skippy peanut butter.

What else? Nothing. It was ready.

They didn't say anything while they ate. Mr. Sabatini put his elbows on the table and leaned down over his plate, so his fork wouldn't have far to go, and put another mouthful in before he swallowed the first. When he had eaten every speck of food, he scraped up the crispy bits from the bottom of the pan and asked Dal if he wanted them, holding them out to him. When Dal shook his head, he ate them straight from the spatula.

Probably not everybody liked corned beef hash and eggs, but Dal and Mr. Sabatini did. He sure can cook, Dal thought, looking at his stepfather. None of his friends' fathers could, as far as he knew.

For dessert they had two Hostess cupcakes apiece with melting vanilla ice cream on top. Since the ice cream was still too big to fit in the freezing compartment, they finished it off.

Afterward they just sat there for a couple of minutes, feeling the way you do after you've eaten your first meal in a new place: like you've really arrived.

They had remembered to buy a bottle of green dish soap, but there was nothing to scour the pot and pan with. "Start a list—two lists," his stepfather said, rolling up his sleeves. "Things to buy and things to do. Here." He tore a page from his pocket notebook and let Dal use his fountain pen, while he washed the dishes, piling everything to dry on the draining board. Dal wrote, "~~scowering skauer~~ pad, sponge, towel. Buy hats. Wash the truck."

Outside in the courtyard there were cool metal chairs. You couldn't be sure what color they were even when Mr. Sabatini switched on the feeble outside light. They sat in the chairs for half an hour or so, without saying much, while Mr. Sabatini smoked one of his cigarillos and Dal jumped up every three minutes to catch fireflies. Every time either of them remembered something else they needed, Dal carefully wrote it down on the list. After a while neither of them could keep from yawning, so they went back inside.

Dal still felt funny about having the one bed all to himself, but Mr. Sabatini said again that he preferred the davenport. "Scout's honor," he said, holding up three fingers. "That way I won't wake you if I get up in the middle of the night. Once the work starts, I'll be up and out of here before dawn. You may want to sleep in."

"I thought I was coming with you."

"Tomorrow you are. Tomorrow you have to meet everyone. But once we get started, it's going to be hard work. You may want to stay here and play."

Or go horseback riding, Dal thought.

He put on his summer pajamas and got into bed. Although he was tired, he couldn't sleep for a long time. Through the gauze curtains in the window, the sign of the Flying Red Horse cast a red glow. Trucks ground by on the highway, less than a block away— *yeeeaaarrrm*—their shadows laboring across the ceiling. He wondered how his mom and Kate were getting along back in Detroit, and whether his mom was still reading *The Princess and the Goblin*, even though he wasn't there to hear it, too. But then he saw the face of his clock glowing in the dark and realized that people in Detroit had gone to bed long ago. If it was seven minutes after ten in Idaho, it was after midnight in Michigan, because on the train he had had to set his watch back twice. I'm out West, Dal thought, trying to take it in.

CHAPTER 5

HAZELTON

The next day they got up late and, after breakfast, drove to Hazelton, five miles east of Eden. Hazelton looked more like a real western town, its totem pole of signs pointing every which way. If Eden was a line, Hazelton was a square, and in fact, there was a square in the small downtown. Three sides of it were taken up with stores—dime store, feed store, drugstore, post office—but the fourth side, shady under old trees, was a city park with a swing set, a teeter-totter, a slide, and a merry-go-round. High above everything else stood the water tower, with HAZELTON painted in bulging letters on its fat belly. The morning was already hot and dry, with a taste of dust and sagebrush in the air.

As Mr. Sabatini pulled into one of the angled parking spaces, Dal eyed the swing set and wondered when, if ever, he was going to meet someone his age.

"Why are the sidewalks so high?" Dal asked. He had discovered that one way to have a conversation with his stepfather was to ask him questions.

"That's the sign of a real western town," Mr. Sabatini replied. "Left over from the cowboy days when people went everywhere on horseback. They could dismount right on the sidewalk and never get their feet wet."

"Where're we going?" Dal asked as they got out and slammed their doors in unison.

"You'll see." Mr. Sabatini neatly hoisted himself up onto the raised sidewalk and went into a shop without waiting for Dal. Mr. Sabatini was a natural-born athlete, or at least that's what Dal's mom said. He was the champion of his bowling league and played second base on the recreation department's baseball team. In the early evenings he would sometimes hit fly balls for Dal and his friends at the playground behind Clark School. Dal was pretty average at sports, not a lard butt like Larry Wiedenhof, who always had the most expensive equipment but couldn't catch a beach ball if you threw underhand. But not a star, either—not like Jimmy Beard, who somersaulted after balls and came up with them in the pocket of his glove. Sometimes Dal wondered if Mr. Sabatini would have been happier with Jimmy Beard for his stepson.

He put his hands on the warm concrete, which came chest high on him, took a couple of practice jumps, and then jumped for real, boosting himself up at the same time—*unh*—and scrambling to his feet. He looked to see if Mr. Sabatini was watching him, but the window was too dark to tell.

A muted jingle greeted Dal as he closed the door behind him. Inside, it was quiet and cool and smelled of new leather. Breathing deeply, Dal looked around. It had everything a real cowboy could need: shirts, boots, harnesses, even saddles mounted on wooden horses. Plus hats galore. Mr. Sabatini was standing in front of a mirror, trying one on. "What do you think?" he asked Dal, who had come up behind him.

"You look like a cowboy," Dal said.

The salesgirl, her arms folded, watched with her head cocked to one side.

"We'll need something for the boy, too," Mr. Sabatini said. "See something you like, Dal?"

"I want a ten-gallon hat!" He didn't know what was funny about that, but when the others laughed, he did, too, so they would think he had said it on purpose.

The salesgirl stood on her tiptoes and hit at the stack of cowboy hats on the top shelf. When they came tumbling down, she managed to catch them, still together. Pulling out the one on the bottom, she handed it to Dal. It was like a headache, too tight.

"This one?" she said, peeling off the one on top, but it sank over his eyes.

The third one, though, was just right. In the mirror he looked like a boy movie star.

Back outside in the sunshine, Dal felt funny to be wearing a hat with such a big brim. It sounded crinkly, like a picnic basket. He sure hoped the other kids wore them, but he didn't see any other kids. Using his hand to steady himself, Mr. Sabatini dropped from the high sidewalk to the street in one neat motion. Dal sat down and jumped the rest of the way, stinging his feet. In the truck he remembered to say thank you.

"Don't mention it," said Mr. Sabatini, starting up the engine. "Out here you need protection from the sun."

Next they drove to the warehouse of the Purity Seed Company, on the edge of town, where a man named Art dumped eight bean bags in the back of the pickup. Each bag was so heavy that it made the truck bounce and sag. "They're for the girls," Mr. Sabatini commented. "They have to sit somewhere, and we try to make things as comfortable for them as we can."

The girls?

They went inside to get a drink. It was cool and quiet in the warehouse, like in the big church they sometimes went to in downtown Detroit. Their footsteps echoed dully as they crossed the empty floor. The pop machine was over by the stairs. You lifted the lid, found the flavor you wanted by the bottle cap, and maneuvered the neck of the bottle along a narrow metal slot to a metal latch. Mr. Sabatini gave Dal a nickel, and he chose root beer. The bottle came up with a crunching sound.

They went back out in the blazing sun. "Say, what do you think of them Commie spies?" Art said, shutting the heavy warehouse doors. "Giving our secret formula to the Russians like that. If you ask me, the electric chair is too good for them."

Mr. Sabatini took off his new hat and scratched his head. "I can't figure out what would make somebody want to betray their country. Think they were brainwashed?"

Dal sat in the pickup to finish his pop, while the two men yakked about Communism. Why didn't Mr. Sabatini have any trouble talking to grown-ups? Dal wondered. After a while his elbow accidentally bumped the horn.

"Oops, somebody's getting restless," said Mr. Sabatini. He fished his keys out of his pocket. "Be seeing you, Art."

They ran some other errands, ate a sandwich, and drove back to the motel so Mr. Sabatini could take a nap. Dal didn't feel like taking a nap, so while Mr. Sabatini lay on the davenport and snored away, he sat quietly at the kitchen table, writing down the formula for the atom bomb. Every once in a while he looked at Mr. Sabatini to see if he was awake yet. *"How did you do it, Professor Wilkins?" "Well, I figured that if* $E=MC^2$ *and you mixed in a lot of radioactive particles, the result was bound to be a chain reaction." He wore a bow tie and smoked a pipe, like the scientists he had seen on TV. "As a token of our appreciation, we would like to offer you this check for one million dollars." His mom and Mr. Sabatini were sitting in the front row, clapping with all their might.*

The next time Dal looked, Mr. Sabatini's eyes were open wide. He rolled off the davenport and said, "Come on. We gotta wash the truck. Big do at the Fosters' tonight. They've invited the girl next door specially to meet you."

Oh, brother, thought Dal.

Mrs. Pucket was weeding her garden. She sat back on her haunches. Yes, they could use her hose if they were careful not to take any more water than they absolutely needed. "Water's precious."

Mr. Sabatini handed the hose to Dal. "Let 'er have it."

"Even the bean sacks?"

"They'll dry."

The pickup was dirty everywhere a truck can be dirty, and it wasn't just regular dirty like a car but coated with dirt, caked with dirt. Dal stood on the running board in his bare feet and used a big soapy sponge to scrub the roof of the cab. He rinsed it with water from the hose, to see how he was doing.

Mr. Sabatini used a pair of his old undershorts ("These have seen better days") to rub away the water spots. He picked up the hose. "There's a place, on the right fender. Lower. Lower." He pointed with his chin.

"Here?"

"No, there!" He let Dal have it with the hose. "Ha-ha!" he laughed. The water scalded Dal, it was so cold. Without stopping to think, he charged Mr. Sabatini and grabbed the hose from his hands.

"Water's precious!" Mr. Sabatini squealed. "We don't want to waste it!"

They were both soaking. They took turns in the shower, Mr. Sabatini going first. He sang in a foreign language at the top of his lungs, "O Sole Mio," whatever that meant. Suddenly he stopped singing, and for about two seconds just hummed. Then he shouted, *"Ow, ow, ow, ow, ow, ow!"* In less than a minute the door opened, and he stepped through a cloud of steam, with a towel around his waist.

"I always turn the hot water off for a minute or two," he said, grinning. "Cold water invigorates your internal organs, helps you live longer. Your turn."

Dal left his wet clothes in a pile on the bathroom floor and got into the metal shower stall. It was like being inside a drum. As he shampooed his hair, he sang "Stranger in Paradise" as loud as he could. He wondered if Mr. Sabatini could hear him over the noise of the water and, if so, whether he thought he was a good singer (how could you tell?). Once Dal got in a hot shower, he never wanted to get out, especially not to go to a picnic where they had invited the girl next door. Maybe she would turn out to be the girl on the train; maybe unbeknownst to him Kay St. John spent her summers in Idaho.

He stayed in the shower until the steam was so thick he could barely see. Then he nonchalantly turned the left-hand knob clockwise as far as it would go. For one and a half seconds—*girl on the train one, Kay St. J*—nothing happened. Then, as the icy stream cascaded over his back, he danced around like an Indian, shouting, *"Ow, ow, ow!"* He couldn't tell if his internal organs were invigorated or not. He felt around quick for the right-hand knob and twisted it to off.

He expected Mr. Sabatini to say something like "That's the ticket!" But when he opened the bathroom door, he saw that his stepdad was outside in the courtyard, talking to Mrs. Pucket. He was wearing his new hat and . . . cowboy boots! Where had he gotten those? They made him look taller. Dal ran into his bedroom with just a towel around his waist and got out his favorite shirt—it had blue checks on it. Mr. Sabatini said he should wear a clean pair of blue jeans. Dal rolled the cuffs up exactly two times. He didn't want people to think he was a square.

Mr. Sabatini rapped on the screen door. "You coming or what?"

THE GIRL NEXT DOOR

Mr. Sabatini said Dal could ride in the back if he wanted to. He stood up most of the way, his legs apart, not holding on unless he had to. He had tried sitting on one of the bean sacks, but they were still sopping wet. Halfway to Hazelton they passed the EAST-OF-EDEN RANCH, ED DUNN PROPRIETOR, where there were horses grazing in a pasture. A greenwillow growing by the fence spilled its long, stringy branches onto cars and trucks that passed beneath. Dal reached out to grab a switch of leaves, but the branches wouldn't break, and before letting go, he got a rope burn on his hand. Why did he do dumb things like that sometimes?

Dal didn't want the ride to end because he knew he would have to meet a lot of people he didn't know—and the seat of his pants was still damp. Unfortunately Mr. Sabatini knew the way. On the outskirts of Hazelton he pulled up to an ordinary-looking driveway, past some bushes and an old farmhouse, and—out into the country again. They parked beside the barn, between another pickup and a tractor. Beyond the farm buildings, a cornfield was being irrigated. The long rows of water were the color of the clear blue sky.

If Kate had been there, he could have said, "See, down there is town, with houses and front yards and sidewalks, like where we live, but this is the country. We don't have chickens in town, do we?" There really were some chickens pecking at the gravel. If Kate had been there, he wouldn't have been the only kid.

He jumped down from the truck, neatly, in case the girl next door happened to be looking out one of the quiet windows of the house. A sheep dog came through the bushes to bark at them: *roof, roof, roof.*

Mr. Sabatini was in a good mood. "That's Sheppy," he said. "She's seventeen years old, if you can believe it. In dog years that's well over a hundred. Good girl. Remember me?"

Sheppy sniffed his hand and then came over to Dal. You could tell she was old from the white whiskers on her thin face. When Dal knelt to pet her, she licked his face.

He wished he could pet the dog forever, but Mr. Sabatini said, "Come and meet everybody." They walked along the side of the house, an old-fashioned two-story building, painted a light blue. Mr. Sabatini said it was one of the oldest houses in that part of Idaho— "built in the 1890s." The picnic was being set up in front of the Fosters' house, which was more like a town park than most people's front yards. Dal still hadn't figured out what an acre was, but he bet their lawn was at least an acre, maybe two. An irrigation ditch divided it in half, forking around some old trees to make an island. Trees grew everywhere, big old shady ones. Dal wanted to jump across the ditch and climb one of them.

He had checked his rear end so many times he couldn't tell anymore if it was damp or not, but there wasn't any girl there anyway.

Before he could go exploring, a short lady came out of the screened-in porch, carrying an enormous platter of cut-up vegetables. She set it down on one of the two long wooden tables in front of the house, wiped her hands on her apron, and shook hands first with Mr. Sabatini and then with Dal. It was Mrs. Foster. Her hair was coiled in ropes on her head. She talked and laughed and ordered people around—but in a nice way.

A man appeared around the side of the house in muddy boots. He smiled shyly. When Mr. Sabatini saw him, his face lit up. "Dal," he said, clapping his hand into the other man's, "I want you to meet Jerry Foster, the best seedsman west of Chicago."

When it was Dal's turn to shake his hand, Mr. Foster glanced at him, but all he said was: "That's quite a grip you have there, partner."

"Land's sake, Jerry," Mrs. Foster said with her hands on her hips. "Hurry up and get dressed before the other guests start arriving. Dal, you come with me. You can help me carry the drinks."

The screened-in porch had piles of old newspapers on the floor. About a million cats were climbing around, and there were more cats in the living room. It was hard to breathe in there. Some of the cats rubbed their backs against his legs; others scampered away and hid behind the sofas and the chairs. Dal knelt on the braided rug and petted the friendliest one. It was orange. Mrs. Foster said its name was Rusty. Instead of getting drinks, she plopped down in an armchair and started fanning her face with her own hand. At least four cats jumped up in her lap. Another one climbed along the back of the chair. Mrs. Foster petted them all and kissed them and asked Dal what grade he was in, how he liked Idaho, and if he missed his mother.

Dal hadn't been thinking about his mother that much, but now that he did, he could just see her all dressed up for a party like this— and he wished she was here, too. She was pretty when she got dressed up, and she smelled good. But all he said was: "Yeah, I guess."

"I'll bet you like your new stepdad," she said. Dal didn't know what to say, so he didn't say anything. "Jerry looks forward all year to his coming out here." She cupped her hand to her mouth like she was going to tell him a secret. "When they get together, they're like a couple of overgrown boys," she said, and laughed her nice laugh.

Dal didn't get it—they were men, not boys—but to be polite, he laughed, too.

Mrs. Foster said that the last time she counted they had seventeen cats. "The house would be so empty without them." For a second she looked sad. Then, getting to her feet, she called out, "You wait here." In about ten seconds she was back with a tray of drinks, which Dal carried very c a r e f u l l y outside and set on one of the tables. He ate a carrot and a celery stick and a green onion. He had never eaten a green onion before, but all of sudden he wanted to see what one tasted like. It crunched in his mouth and tasted cool and hot at the same time, so he ate another one, loitering by the table. Mr. Foster and his stepdad were over by the driveway, talking to another man Dal didn't know. Mr. Foster had pulled his boots off and was standing in his stocking feet. Dal could have gone over—Mr. Sabatini would have introduced him, and he could have listened to what they were saying—but across the lawn fireflies glimmered under trees. Mrs. Foster came out with a basket of rolls. "Supper's almost ready," she said in a low voice. "Run over to Patty's house and tell her it's time to eat."

Since nobody had said anything about the girl next door, Dal hoped that maybe they had forgotten about her, but now his heart was beating. But he didn't want Mrs. Foster to know he was shy, so he said, "Where does she live?"

"Go past the lilac bushes"—she turned him in the right direc-tion—"into the street. Patty lives in the second brick house. It has green awnings. Just stand in the driveway and holler, 'Patty!' She'll come."

Oh, brother, Dal thought, marching to his doom. He took the long way around so that he had to jump over two ditches. He lingered as long as he could in the lilac bushes, holding bunches of the blossoms to his nose. Then he forced his way through into the ordinary-looking street.

As he emerged from the bushes, a girl came down the driveway of the brick house with the green awnings. She waved when she saw him and ran right up to him. "Hi, Dal," she said.

He didn't know what to say, so he said hi back.

"I just about always eat over at their place," she said, falling in beside him. "Because my parents are divorced. They can't have children of their own, the Fosters—isn't that sad? They've sort of adopted me. Me and the cats." She ducked under the lilac bushes on a well-beaten path, and he followed. "Did you see how many cats they have? Eighteen."

"Seventeen," said Dal.

Patty stopped. "That's right. Tiger died. Oh."

When she said, "Oh," her pale blue eyes suddenly filled with tears, but she kept on smiling. She had freckles and reddish blond hair, and she was wearing pedal pushers with red sandals, plus she had on one of those too-small tops. You could see her tummy and belly button even without looking. When some tears started dripping down her cheeks, she shook her head impatiently and used the fat part of her palms to rub them away. Even without exactly looking at her, Dal could see everything she did, and he could see himself, too. He had left his body and was flying around overhead, spying on them below.

When they got to the ditch, she put her hand on him, to undo the straps on her sandals, which she threw across the ditch with all her might. Then, backing up to get a running start, she jumped over. It was only about a yard wide, but her heel landed on the edge of the grass, and she started making windmills with her arms. Dal jumped over and grabbed her arm to steady her. She was laughing. He stood still, so she could hold on to put her sandals back on, first one foot, then the other.

"How old are you?" Dal asked.

"Eleven. Why, how old are you?"

Her birthday was in October, his in August. He was two months and six days older. As they came walking up to the house, some lady said, "Don't they look cute together?" Dal felt his face grow hot. He went over to the glass that had onion stems sticking out of it and grabbed a handful. Patty was going around to all the grown-ups, saying, "Hi, Jerry," "Hi, Miz Knoop."

Dal caught up with her and chomped an onion right in her face. "You want one?"

"I don't dare. My breath will stink."

"Does mine?" Dal said, breathing on her.

She wrinkled her nose. "You smell nice," she said, taking one of the onions after all. He watched her put it in her mouth. It was a very ordinary thing to do—everybody eats—but when Patty chewed and swallowed, it seemed amazing.

A lot of people showed up for the picnic. They parked their cars right on the lawn and bore covered dishes to the already crowded tables. The men joined the other men, and the women joined the women. Mrs. Foster introduced Dal if he was handy. Everybody knew Patty already.

"You can start the line," Mrs. Foster whispered, handing them each a plate. Dal loaded his with fried chicken and potato salad and baked beans and regular salad and homemade bread. He used to think he hated baked beans, and if his salad had dressing on it, he'd spit it in his napkin. But as he and Patty wandered off, eating and talking, he tried everything, and everything was delicious. He stood up tall and put his shoulders back. This was the beginning of his new life as a not-shy boy and a not-finicky eater.

Patty knew where they could sit under the trees.

"When I was little, I used to have tea parties out here with my dolls," she said, sitting on a swing. It was a board big enough for two hanging from the tree by two thick ropes. Patty sat to one side and crossed her ankles. She took dainty bites.

Dal didn't feel like sitting down. He walked in circles, eating with his fingers, bragging and cracking stupid jokes. "A big moron and a little moron were climbing up the hill. The big moron fell off. Why didn't the little moron?"

"Because," said Patty, "he was a little more on. That's the oldest joke in the universe." But she laughed anyway.

There was a commotion, somebody arriving late. A wave of loud talking and laughter spread through the company.

Patty craned her neck to see. Her face was a pale moon.

"Who is it?" said Dal.

Patty shrugged. "My dad."

Mrs. Foster's voice sailed across the lawn. "Patty, your father's here."

Dal carried his empty plate in both hands. He shoved it on the edge of the already crowded table. Mr. Sabatini said, "Dal, I want you to meet an old friend of mine, Leonard Pucket." Pucket? It seemed like everyone around here was named Pucket! Mr. Pucket was holding a greenish bottle of Coca-Cola in one hand and a machine like a battery charger in the other. Before he shook hands with Dal—"Howdy, partner"—he carefully set the machine on the ground. Then he saw Patty and tried to find somewhere to stick the bottle. He would have put it on the table, but the table was stacked with dirty dishes. Finally he just stuck it in the pocket of his overalls and held out his arms as far as they'd go. He was a tall, skinny man with red hair. His face was sunburned, and he had big red hands. He gave Patty a big hug and kiss and said, "Hi, sugarplum."

It seemed to Dal that she wrinkled her nose, but when he looked again, she was smiling at her dad, saying, "Hi, Len," in the same boisterous way he spoke. She had her hands on her hips. Everybody laughed. Dal couldn't believe his ears. None of the kids he knew called their parents by their first names.

Patty came up behind Dal and whispered in his ear: "Let's go play on the swing," but Mr. Pucket must have heard because he called out, "Don't you two go sneaking off yet. I got something I want to show you first." He looked around for the machine he had been carrying and picked it up carefully. "Anybody know what this is?"

Dal did, now that he got a better look. He blurted out, "It's a Geiger counter."

"Hey! There's a smart feller. What'd you say your name was?"

"Dal," said Dal, and for some reason everybody laughed again.

"Now, wait a sec. Lookee here," Mr. Pucket said, taking his bottle out of his pocket. Again he went through the charade of not knowing where to put it. Finally he tipped it over his mouth and took a long swig. He wiped his mouth with the back of his hand, stuck the empty bottle in his armpit, and reached his hand into his back pocket. After a sort of two-step, he pulled out a rock, an ordinary-looking rock, and held it up for everybody to see.

"You're going to tell us you struck gold in that old mine of yours?" somebody said.

"Nope," Mr. Pucket said, smiling. "But my partner here's going to tell you what I did find." And he winked at Dal.

But it wasn't any of the rocks Dal knew. It wasn't mica; it wasn't quartz. Dal felt like he was taking a test, and he was on mental high alert.

Mr. Pucket unhooked the microphone thingy from the Geiger counter and flicked the switch. Immediately the machine made a staticky sound. The crickets quieted down to listen. When he held the rock up to the mike, the machine went *click, click, click.*

"It's uranium!" Dal shouted.

Nobody else said anything, but Mr. Pucket nodded. "He's right. One hundred percent pure u-ran-i-um." He pronounced it carefully, in syllables, as if it was a big word he had just memorized. The clicks from the Geiger counter filled the empty spaces of the night. While everybody watched and listened, he fished another stone out of his pocket. He beckoned to Dal to come up and try it and handed him the mike. The second piece made the machine click louder than the first.

"Try this," said Mr. Foster, handing Dal a stone from beside the house. He held it up to the machine, but nothing happened. They tried to fool the Geiger counter with other objects: a fork, somebody's wedding ring, a Zippo lighter. Each time the machine seemed to scent the object. Each time there was a loud, staticky moment of suspense. But no clicks—until Mr. Foster showed it his watch. Then, the telltale *click, click, click.* The watch had a radium dial.

"How does it work?" somebody asked, taking the machine from Len's hands and holding it up so he could peer at its bottom.

Len looked at Dal. Dal shrugged. Uranium and radium were radioactive. That meant they emitted particles smaller than atoms. But how a Geiger counter knew that—how exactly it picked them up—was beyond him. He bet Miss Howe, his sixth-grade teacher, knew.

Dal wanted to go exploring with the Geiger counter to see if he could find more uranium, but Len said, "We'd better turn her off now."

Mrs. Foster, with her arms out, piloted Dal and Patty to the table laden with dishes. It was fun to see how many dirty plates and glasses and knives and forks you could carry at once around the side of the house and straight into the kitchen, where there were already piles by the sink. It took about six trips. Some ladies helped, too.

Dal said, "Your dad's funny."

"Len? He's a riot."

Mrs. Foster said they were through. "I'll call you when the dessert's ready."

"Come on, let's go," Patty said, but Dal wanted to hang around and hear what else Len had to say. They were discussing the atom bomb, and at one point Len lifted his hands to fashion a mushroom cloud out of thin air.

Patty came up behind Dal again and bumped him hard. This time she was carrying two huge helpings of apple pie and ice cream. He followed her back to their "island," where they sat on the bare ground, with their backs against a tree.

"Want a fork?" Patty said. Two forks were sticking out the top of her pedal pushers like flowers.

The apples were still warm; the crust was thick and sweet. A humpback moon was shining through the leaves.

"Did your father really discover a uranium mine?" Dal asked.

"Probably," Patty said, her mouth full of pie.

"Wow," said Dal. "That's worth a lot of money."

"A fortune," said Patty, chewing.

Dal looked at her.

She swallowed and said, "We've been rich before. My mom says we were once the richest family in Jerome County."

"What happened?"

"Len drank half and gambled the rest away." She sounded like she was quoting someone. "The Fosters are building a bomb shelter," she added.

"They are? Why?"

"In case there's a atom bomb. We can live down there for six months."

"Can we see it?"

Patty scrunched her face up and squinted at the grown-ups milling around in front of the house. "Better not. I'm not supposed to go down there. I've seen it, though. They're going to have a cot for me." Her knees were drawn up practically to her chin. She unfastened the straps on her sandals and wiggled her toes.

Since Patty was telling him secrets, Dal wanted to tell her a secret, too. "My stepfather's real name is Hercules. Everybody thinks it's Harry."

Patty licked the back of her fork and didn't say anything.

Dal took *his* shoes and socks off and stuffed his socks inside his shoes. He got up and started running in circles under the trees. *"Bombs awaaay!"* he cried, making the sound of an explosion *(ppkugh)*. Fireflies twinkled. He caught one in his hot hand and showed it to Patty, opening his fingers carefully. The bug walked around on his skin, straightening its formal wings. When it turned its light on, his hand glowed.

Mrs. Foster called. They quickly put their shoes back on and ran to the house. Len was sitting on the porch step. There were five or six people sitting around, some on regular wooden chairs that somebody must have lugged from the house. Dal went and stood by his stepdad. Len had on his reading glasses and was holding up an official-looking document. Sometimes glasses made a person look smart, but they made Len look cross-eyed. He was saying something about shares. Dal tried to understand what it was, but he was too excited.

Patty came to say good-night, and the others got up and said they had to leave, too. Patty shook hands with his stepdad. He was scared she would call him Hercules or Harry, but she just said, "Glad to meet you, Mr. Sabatini."

"The pleasure's all mine, Miss Pucket," he said, and laughed like he had said something hilarious.

Patty laughed, too. Dal watched with wonder. She wasn't the least bit shy. He wouldn't have minded having *her* for a stepsister.

Afterward, driving back to Eden, Dal asked Mr. Sabatini if he was going to give money to Len Pucket for his mine.

His stepfather looked at him. "I'll be honest with you. It sure is tempting. The trouble is, he's asking a lot—a hundred bucks. That's practically our groceries for the whole summer."

"We can't then. We need to eat."

Mr. Sabatini snorted. "You're not much of gambler, are you? If he's really struck uranium, anyone who invests stands to earn a small fortune."

Back in the motel, Dal wanted to see what it felt like. Mr. Sabatini called out, "Night," from the other room, and Dal, already under the covers, said, "Good night, Harry." But when a couple of seconds later his stepfather came and stood in the doorway, Dal lay still and watched him.

"Look," Mr. Sabatini said, "I'm a grown man. You're not supposed to call me by my first name. You could call me Dad if you wanted to. That'd be okay."

Dal didn't say anything. He waited for the square silhouette to go away. "Dad," he whispered, but it felt weird. He fell asleep, wondering if and when he would see Patty again.

CHAPTER 7

ROGUING

His stepfather said, "You don't have to get up if you don't want to." Light from the kitchen spilled through the open door. "I can come back at lunchtime and see how you're doing."

"No," said Dal, licking his lips and sitting up. He looked out the window. It was still dark out. The Flying Red Horse was a shadow against the sky. One of these nights he would make himself stay up until they turned it off.

When he walked into the kitchen a few seconds later, Mr. Sabatini was sitting at the table, already dressed in a khaki work shirt and pants, eating soft-boiled eggs from a coffee cup. Dal sat down in the other chair and had a bowl of Rice Krispies. He leaned on his elbow as he ate.

Mr. Sabatini was waiting in the truck. Dal carried his hat in his hand. The morning air was cooler than he expected; he ran back and got a sweatshirt. The engine roared, but the other units remained dark and still. The whole way to Hazelton theirs was the only truck on the road, and when they got there, the town looked empty under its streetlights. They drove to the warehouse.

The men waiting on the loading dock looked like clay statues—only they weren't men: they were women in heavy jackets with their hats pulled down over their foreheads. Mr. Sabatini got out and talked to one of them. Dal got out, too, but stood apart. It was neat to be the only ones up. Not ten blocks from here Patty Pucket was still asleep. Dal wondered if he could find the way to her house. He wondered what kind of pajamas she wore to bed. He always wondered personal things about people, like if they really closed their eyes when they said their prayers.

Mr. Sabatini held his clipboard under the streetlight and read off the names. One by one the women said, "Here," and climbed in the back and sat on the bean sacks. They were big women, seven in all, and some of their names were Lucy, Linda, and Darlene. A couple of them smiled at Dal.

Mr. Sabatini got in on his side, slammed the door, and started the engine, so Dal went around and got in, too. It felt funny to be sitting up front, now that there were seven women he hadn't been introduced to sitting in the back. He felt like the boss's son.

Mr. Sabatini drove with the headlights on. "That's the roguing crew," he said. "One no-show." He glanced at his clipboard on the seat between them. "Bernice Towers. She called in sick, but Lucy says she was out late last night. We're not going to pay anyone who doesn't show up. Makes more work for everyone else."

Dal looked at him. He sounded mad.

His stepfather rolled down the window and spit in the wind. There were cries from the back: "Oh," "It went all over me," "Quit spitting out the window, mister." Somebody pounded angrily on the roof of the cab. Dal tried not to smile. Mr. Sabatini stuck his head and one arm out the window. He tried to say he was sorry, but it wasn't easy, driving down the highway at sixty-five miles per hour. He rolled his window back up and hunched grimly over the steering wheel. Dal turned around to look at the women. Half of them were leaning against one another with their eyes closed.

They drove for maybe half an hour. The stars disappeared; gradually it got light out. Dal's eyes were closing when someone pounded on the back window: bang, bang, bang. Mr. Sabatini waved and, at the next left, turned onto a dirt road. Fifty yards farther on he slowed to a stop and, leaning through his open door, consulted with whoever was giving him directions. With his door still ajar, he drove slowly forward to where a homemade bridge crossed an irrigation ditch into a field. The bridge didn't look strong enough to hold a pickup truck with nine people in it, but a series of encouraging thumps from the back urged him across and up the other side. They drove along the wire fence and parked in the corner of the field under some trees. As soon as the truck stopped, the women climbed down and started walking along the edge of the field.

Dal threw his sweatshirt on the front seat. The sun was up, and it was already warm. He put his new hat on—he wanted to see what people would say.

Mr. Sabatini called out some directions, but the "girls" didn't wait for him. As soon as they reached the corner of the field, they fanned out, one every two rows, and started in among the beans. They walked with measured steps in the narrow trough of dirt between bean rows, reaching over every now and then to pluck up a plant.

Mr. Sabatini watched for a while. Then he said to Dal, "Come on, I'll show you how to rogue. Pick a row and walk all the way to the end. If you spot a plant that's different from the others, pull it up."

"That's *roguing?*"

"It's like weeding, except the rogues are bean plants, too. They could be a different variety that got mixed in by mistake. Or they could be a hybrid. Hybrids are usually bigger than the others—they're easy to spot."

"Is that one?"

"Yep. Make sure you get the whole plant, roots and all."

He followed Dal up the row.

"Why are rogues so bad?"

"Well, because we're in the business of growing seeds for backyard gardens. Our customers want to be able to plant a certain variety of bean—these are called 'Summer's Joy'—and have *it* come up and not something else. No other company goes to as much trouble as Purity does. That's why we're number one. We guarantee the *purity* of our product, get it?"

"What do you do?"

"I'm a crop inspector," Mr. Sabatini said, putting his hands in his back pockets. "I drive the crew to the right field and make sure they get the job done right. Whenever I can, I try to meet with the farmers ahead of time, to reassure them that the company's inspections of their crops are in everybody's best interests. Some of them can get a little hotheaded. They think we're snooping. One year a farmer set his dogs on me. But I get along fine with most of them."

Dal was busy looking for rogues—spies pretending to be good guys. When they came to the end of a row, they tossed the plants they'd been carrying into the heap the women had already started, turned and began a new row. It was slow, monotonous work. In an hour the crew had covered only a fraction of the field. They sat down in the shade of the trees (aspens, Mr. Sabatini told Dal, showing him a jagged leaf). Some of them washed their faces in the irrigation ditch or drank water out of their hands.

Dal followed his stepfather over to where they were sitting. "That's a good pace," Mr. Sabatini announced in too loud a voice. He sounded like a gym teacher. "We'll have a ten-minute rest, then get back to work." Nobody looked at him. He rubbed his hands and smiled, showing all his teeth.

Dal sat down and crossed his legs like in gym.

"Everybody, I'd like to introduce my stepson, Dal."

Someone said, "Hey, Dale."

"Not Dale, Dal, short for Dallas."

"Dallas? Mind if we call you Tex? You look like a Tex in that hat."

"Cut it out, Darlene. He looks cute in that hat."

"We'd prefer you to call him Dal. Dallas is his middle name. That's what he goes by."

Dal felt dumb. Why hadn't they just called him Jimmy or John?

When the ten minutes were up—Mr. Sabatini kept glancing nonchalantly at his watch—the women slowly stood up and walked back among the beans. "Come on, Tex," Darlene said. "You can rogue with us."

Dal looked at Mr. Sabatini. After a second's hesitation his stepfather nodded.

The women bombarded him with questions: What did he want to be when he grew up, what sports did he play, didn't he get bored, hanging around with Hercules all the time?

So the secret was out! They knew Mr. Sabatini's name!

"Look at him stand there like a little Mussolini," Darlene said. "Like we needed someone to tell us what to do."

"Hush," said Lucy, who couldn't help laughing.

Dal didn't say anything, but he felt like a traitor just hearing what they said about his stepfather. Why did they seem to dislike him so much? He didn't shout at them. If anything, he was very polite. For the rest of the morning Dal kept an eye on Mr. Sabatini, who stood alone on the edge of the field or sat in the cab of the pickup with his reading glasses on. He looked lonely.

At twelve o'clock the crew finished the rows they were working on and headed back under the trees. Nobody said, "Time to break for lunch." They just got out their lunches from where they had stored them in the shade. Some of them sat down to eat; others lay on the grass by the irrigation ditch with their arms over their faces and took forty winks. Dal didn't realize how hot and sweaty he was until he sat down, too, next to his stepdad and a little apart from the women. Mr. Sabatini had packed them peanut butter and jelly sandwiches, hard-boiled eggs with salt and pepper twisted up in a piece of wax paper, oranges, and windmill cookies. He stretched out his full length and fished two bottles of pop from the running water and opened them with the little can opener on his pocketknife. They were icy cold.

Before the lunch break was over, some of the women got up and climbed over the wire fence.

Mr. Sabatini looked at his watch. "Excuse me, ladies. Time we were getting back to work. Where they going?"

"They're going to piss," Darlene said, lying on her back with her eyes closed. "And since you two are men—or a man and a boy— they're crossing the road to be dainty and ladylike."

Mr. Sabatini watched them in dismay.

"It would help," said Darlene, her eyes still closed, "if you looked the other way."

Dal tried not to laugh. Darlene sure was funny, but she shouldn't have said p-i-s-s. Dal felt embarrassed when people said swear-words in public. (He sometimes whispered them to himself to see what it felt like.)

"In case you're wondering," Darlene drawled, sitting up and examining a mosquito bite on her arm, "I went before, when nobody was looking. I squatted in some weeds."

"Please!" Mr. Sabatini said. "The boy!"

She deliberately turned to look at the boss in her slow, blinking way but didn't say anything else.

When all the "girls" were back at work, Dal and Mr. Sabatini went off in the truck to look for the farmer who owned the field. It felt strange to drive away and leave the others hard at work, but it was a relief to see some other scenery for a change. Dal was pretty sure he didn't want to work on a roguing crew when he grew up. Hot, dusty air blew in their open windows, making them thirsty again. The country roads all looked alike, and they ended up back on the highway. They stopped at a country store to ask for directions— and share a Nehi—but they never did find the farmer.

From a distance they were just women bent over in the field; then, as they parked the truck under the aspens, they became women he knew, each with her own face. The one he liked best was named Rosanna, a big, strong woman with a nice laugh. Dal walked beside her for the rest of the afternoon. When he found out she lived in

Hazelton, he couldn't resist asking if she knew Patty Pucket, but Rosanna shook her head.

"She lives in Hazelton, too."

"Maybe if I saw her, I'd recognize her. I don't know that many little kids. Kids your age, I mean."

"She has reddish blond hair, she's kind of skinny, she has freckles." He stood still for a second and pushed his hat off his sweaty forehead. "She's nice."

They worked more mechanically in the afternoon, with longer gaps between talking. Dal understood, without anyone telling him, that they were trying to finish off the field before they quit.

Dal felt sorry every time he looked up and saw his stepfather, who had no one to keep him company. But on the way back to Hazelton, when Mr. Sabatini said he could ride in back, if he wanted, Dal eagerly joined the crew. He got to sit on the eighth bean sack. The sudden breeze felt good on his hot skin. He held his hat in his lap so it wouldn't blow onto the highway. His shoulders ached. They drove into a cloudburst. Squealing, the women unfurled a large tarpaulin that was stashed between two bean sacks. It billowed up; they had to haul it back down. Sixteen hands, including Dal's, held it over their heads, a gusty tent. The rain didn't last long. When sunlight spilled over the edges of the clouds, they bunched up the tarp and held it down with their feet. The women starting singing a song about shrimp boats a-comin'. Dal sang, too, trying to learn the words as he went. Even Darlene sang. When she stood up, back at the warehouse, to jump off the back of the truck, she blinked at him about five times. She said, "So long, Tex."

"I've been thinking," Mr. Sabatini said that evening, back at the motel, eating breakfast for supper. "If you're going to do a day's work, you should get paid for it."

Dal pricked up his ears. "How much?"

"Well, that's what you and I need to settle. The girls get seventy-five cents an hour. I watched you out there. You work almost as hard as they do, but you're underage, and you're the boss's son—well, stepson, same difference. How about fifty cents?"

"You don't have to pay me," Dal said, getting up to fetch the ice cream.

"I'm going to bring it up when I see Jerry tomorrow. It's only fair. If you saved up—eight hours a day most days, five days a week—at the end of a week you'd have twenty dollars."

Dal tried not to smile.

They moved outside, onto the metal chairs. While Mr. Sabatini smoked, Dal licked the inside of the ice cream container. He wondered how much a TV cost. *"Keep your eyes shut,"* he would say, *leading his mom by the hand into the living room. "What is it?" "Oh, I can't wait." "It's a TV!" Kate would shout. "Yep, it's a Zenith. I bought it with my own money."*

CHAPTER 8

YOU'RE FIRED!

Dal imagined he had a horse and a friend who also had a horse. *They rode like the wind until they came through aspens to a stream. Dal swung down from the saddle and let the reins hang loose. He unpacked his saddlebags and started a fire. His friend was a boy he hadn't met yet, his face lost in the shade, a better friend than he had ever had. Or it was Jimmy Beard; he was Jimmy's guide and scout. "This is Idaho," Dal would say, making a sweeping gesture with his ten-gallon hat.*

Sometimes it was Patty Pucket, dressed like a cowgirl. She rode behind him with her arms around his waist and laughed at all his jokes.

"A penny for your thoughts," Rosanna said.

"Huh?" said Dal.

"You were smiling about something."

Dal felt his face turn red. "He promised to take me horseback riding, but he hasn't yet."

"Oh," said Rosanna, stooping over to yank out a rogue.

When he said "he," Dal nodded at his stepfather, who was doing jumping jacks under a cottonwood tree. Oh, brother. He often did calisthenics right out in the open where everyone could see.

How much did a horse cost anyway? Dal kept adding up the money he was making. This was his second week. By Friday he would have over thirty dollars. By the end of the summer he would have well over a hundred. A hundred dollars was a fortune—and a lot of responsibility. Maybe he should invest some of it in Len Pucket's uranium mine. *Dal Wilkins, the richest boy in America. "How did you to it, Master Wilkins?" "Call me Dal. Oh, I worked hard. I'm also a bit of a gambler."*

Then, just when he thought he was getting good at roguing, Mr. Sabatini fired him. They were driving back to the motel Friday evening when it happened. At first Dal wasn't even paying that close attention. He had his pay packet in his pocket: two crisp ten-dollar bills. Mr. Sabatini was going on about how "some of the girls" objected to him because he was so young. They complained that he took work away from them.

"It doesn't help that you're related to the boss."

"What does that have to do with it?"

"I'm not real popular with the girls, don't ask me why. They ever say anything to you about me?"

Dal, the traitor, shrugged and shook his head.

"Guess they figure if we're going to have a ninth roguer, it should be one of the girls Jerry passed over when he was hiring in May. We're only talking about two or three troublemakers. The others don't seem to care one way or the other."

"So what am I supposed to do now?" Dal whined. "Stay in the crummy motel all day?"

Mr. Sabatini frowned at him. "I'm sorry it has to be this way, Dal, but that's life, I'm afraid. You're going to have to act grown-up about it."

"But you're the boss!" Dal wailed. "You can tell people to jump in the lake if you want to. Why don't you fire Judy Clark? I can rogue ten times faster than she can. Or Darlene. You're always saying she's the real troublemaker. You're firing me because—because you're afraid of her, but you're not afraid of me."

Dal could hardly believe those words had come out of his mouth. But they had. And for about five seconds he was glad they had.

Mr. Sabatini's ears were red. "That's enough, Dal. I already get grief from the girls, some of them. I don't need you to turn against me, too."

Dal squeezed his face as hard as he could. He didn't want Mr. Sabatini to see him cry. But a few tears dripped down his cheeks anyway. He quickly wiped them away.

As soon as they pulled up in front of Unit Number 4, Dal jumped out and slammed his door as hard as he could. Unfortunately he had to wait while Mr. Sabatini fumbled with his keys, but as soon as the door was open, he ran to his room and flopped down on his bed, setting all the springs in motion: *boing, boing, boing.* He expected his stepfather to follow; he was relieved and disappointed when he didn't. He could hear him moving quietly in the other room.

He had thought the "girls" liked him. He had felt part of the crew. Who else (besides Darlene) could have complained? He hated Darlene's guts, but the others all seemed so friendly. He pictured spending the rest of the summer in the stupid motel with nothing to do. He wrote Patty a letter in his head. *Dear Patty, I lost my job. I don't know when, if ever, I'll get to come to Hazelton, again. Sincerely, Dal.* Or *Love, Dal.* A good thing he hadn't told anybody about his secret plan to invest in the uranium mine because he wouldn't have enough money now.

Mr. Sabatini tapped on the door and opened it a crack. "Want to eat out?"

"I'm not hungry."

"I feel like fried chicken."

Dal thought of saying, "You go," but the mention of food made his stomach growl. He rolled off the bed and went to wash his face.

They were walking in the warm evening. "I've been thinking," his stepfather said.

Dal braced himself.

"You know, you don't have to stay in the motel all day. You

could help me drive around and meet the farmers. It's easier if one of us drives and the other navigates. I could teach you to read the map. It would save me time. I'd still pay you."

"That's all right," Dal said. "You don't have to pay me."

Mr. Sabatini held the screen door and followed him inside the Two Spud, Eden's one and only cafe. That was its gimmick: you got two orders of potatoes with every meal. You could have mashed with french fries or baked with mashed or just two mashed, like a gravy-covered mountain range.

It was hot in there. Two fans the size of bomber propellers strained against their pivots but barely stirred the greasy air. Dal slid into an empty booth, and when the waitress brought them ice water with their menus, he drank his straight down and asked if he could have some more, please. His forehead was sweaty.

"You all know what you want?" the waitress said, fanning herself with their menus before plunking them down. "Them fans ain't helpin', in case you hadn't noticed." You could see the pores on her sweaty nose.

"I'll have a grilled cheese and a chocolate malt," Dal said, flipping the selection cards of the miniature jukebox above the table.

"You could have the fried chicken," his stepfather suggested. "Or the daily special. You like meat loaf and mashed potatoes with gravy."

"And french fries."

"I have another idea," Mr. Sabatini said when they were alone again. "You know how you keep saying you want to go horseback riding? That farm we pass every day on the way to Hazelton? They have horses. Mr. Dunn, the farmer, grows beans for us. He has a son about your age."

Dal felt his shoulders hunch.

"Margaret Foster says there's a pool in Twin Falls. Twice a week a bus picks up kids from Hazelton and Eden and takes them swimming. I happen to know that Mr. Dunn's boy goes. All I'm saying is there are other things to do around here besides roguing beans in the hot sun.

"Think about it," he said after the waitress had brought them their suppers. "We could drive over to the Dunns' next Monday and meet them. When I found out about the, er . . . trouble with the girls, I took the liberty of giving Mr. Dunn a call. He said *he* has no objection if you want to stay over there a couple of nights."

"Stay over! I don't even know them."

"Well, I know that, but they're good, hardworking people. Mr. Dunn doesn't say much. His wife seems pretty nice. Like I say, we could drive over Monday morning, see what you think. You could give me a signal or something, if you wanted to stay."

"I guess," Dal said, licking his long spoon.

9

HOME ALONE

The next morning Dal slept late and, when he woke up, found half a banana with a note on the kitchen table.

SAT. A.M. I'M GOING TO BE IN MEETINGS ALL DAY. HERE'S THE KEY — DON'T LOSE IT. SEE YOU IN THE P.M. IF YOU NEED ANYTHING, ASK MRS. PUCKET. HARRY SABATINI, YOUR "DAD"

Dal sliced the banana into a bowl of Wheaties. After breakfast he put on the same clothes he'd worn the day before. From his private suitcase under the bed, the one that he had packed himself, he got out the book he had started on the train. He went out into the court-yard, where Conchita, the chambermaid, was pushing her cart of fresh sheets and pillowcases from unit to unit. She had a purple birthmark on one side of her face, but she was nice. He waved to her; she said something in Spanish and waved back. It was already hot in the drive. Dal dragged one of the metal chairs over to the grass where there was a little shade from the motel sign and sat down.

He opened the book to page one; he had to start over because he could hardly remember anything from the time on the train. He had read about two pages when Mrs. Pucket yoo-hooed him from her garden. "Want some wild strawberries?" she said, holding up a teacup.

"That's all right," said Dal, kicking the front of the chair.

"Well, come and get them," Mrs. Pucket said. "You have young legs, so you can walk over here easier than I can over there."

Dal remembered she was hard-of-hearing. Sighing, he marked his page and marched over. Mrs. Pucket held the cup over the fence, and Dal picked a strawberry and put it in his mouth. Its sharp sweetness surprised him.

"Take them all," Mrs. Pucket said, waggling the cup at him. "Your daddy told me you'd be here by yourself today. Why don't you read in the garden instead of out there where it's so hot? I like to see a boy read. My son never had any use for books. All he ever thinks about is making money."

Dal felt like saying he didn't read *that* much. At home his mom always read to him after he got ready for bed. He liked climbing into bed beside her and listening to the story—she had a different voice for each of the characters. But now that Kate lived with them, his mom had to read to her, too. She tried to pick books that they both would like, but there weren't that many. If the book was the least bit hard, Kate started squirming off the side of the bed, dragging the covers with her and giggling. If the book was too babyish or more for girls, Dal moved out in the hall, taking a book of his own with him, so no one would know if he was listening or not.

Mrs. Pucket was beaming at him. She acted as if she was *proud* of him for reading. (She had probably been a schoolteacher before getting into the motel business.) After politely asking permission, Dal climbed up into one of the apricot trees, settled in a fork of some branches, and opened his book to where he had left off. If he was getting a reputation as a reader, he might as well earn it.

Through the screen of her kitchen window Mrs. Pucket called out, "Now don't fall down and break your leg like my son did once." A few minutes later her shadowy face appeared again. "I plugged in the radio so we can listen to some music." Even from where Dal was sitting, the volume was way too loud, with static and humming probably from another planet. They played that song about the shrimp boats, and Dal sang along under his breath. Mrs. Pucket came out with a wicker basket full of wet sheets and began pegging them to the clothesline.

"Don't mind me," she said. "You go right on with your reading."

Dal liked the book all right. Young Ralph Moody didn't have to stay at a stupid motel all day. He lived on a ranch, rode horses, and had adventures. But it's hard to pay attention when someone keeps watching you.

He kept his nose in his book until she went back in the house. Then he slipped out of the tree and went and sat in a lawn chair where no one could see him. The chair was set too low, but he was afraid if he tried to adjust it, it would come apart and he wouldn't know how to put it back together again.

He found his place again, and the next time he looked up, he had read to page 35. Wow. Mr. Sabatini would come home and find the book with the bookmark sticking out of it on the kitchen table. "You read all this?" he would say. "I guess," Dal would say nonchalantly.

Dal wondered if he could read the whole book before his step-father got home, but doubted it, since it had taken him all morning to read to page 35.

Mrs. Pucket came back out, carrying a tray. "I fixed us some lunch," she said.

It was sandwiches, already made, so he couldn't say no, plus he was starving. But what if she had put mayonnaise on the bread? But she hadn't. He lifted up one corner to make sure. They were peanut butter and apricot jam sandwiches, with lemonade in a scratched-up, green plastic glass.

As he bit into the sandwich, the music on the radio stopped, and a news bulletin came on. In a very dramatic high voice, the announcer said that yesterday evening, just before sunset, Julius and Ethel

Rosenberg had been taken from their cells in Sing Sing and led to the execution chamber, where first Julius and then Ethel had been put to death in the electric chair. Frantic last-minute appeals to the President had proved futile. The prison warden, in an exclusive *live* interview, said that both prisoners appeared subdued. Julius wore a white T-shirt and cloth slippers; he had shaved off his mustache. He was strapped to the chair; the electrodes were attached. "Could you describe the actual chair?" the interviewer interrupted to ask. The warden didn't say anything for a second. "Well," he said, "it's just an old chair really. Nothing special. It's brown." As soon as the leather hood was dropped over Julius's face, three shocks of two thousand volts were sent through his body.

They had just removed his corpse when Ethel was led into the room. She gave her matron a quick kiss on the cheek. Her hair had been cut short to make the electrical apparatus fit better. Three shocks of two thousand volts were administered. The attending doctors rushed forward. They thought they detected a faint heartbeat, so two more shocks were given, after which she was pronounced dead.

Supporters of the convicted pair said that it was a dark day for our country. You could hear a crowd in the background, and one woman shouting that America was worse than Nazi Germany. But a woman on the street said it was time the government rounded up all the Commie spies—"unless they've already infiltrated the government," she said.

Dal's mouth was full of peanut butter, and for a second he felt like he was choking—he made gulping motions like a dog and couldn't swallow. He reached for his glass of lemonade. His heart was racing. Mrs. Pucket got up and went inside to turn off the radio. When she came back, she had a fresh pitcher of lemonade.

She refilled Dal's glass. He squeaked, "Thank you." He wondered what it felt like to be executed. One minute you were alive, and then—what exactly? Did you go straight to heaven, or did everything go blank, like a TV screen, with just a white dot that finally popped? Being dead was probably like before you were born, and nobody was horrified that before August 16, 1941, John D. Wilkins, Jr., didn't exist, except in his mother's tummy. Only now that you knew how good it was to be alive, who would want to go back in time?

Dal's real dad knew the answers to these questions. Sometimes Dal wished he could call him up and ask him what it was like. He wondered if his dad would know it was him on the other end. *It's me, Dal, your son. I'll be twelve in August.* At the top of the stairs at home hung a photograph of Jack Wilkins with his army buddies. They were piled in a jeep with their arms crossed, laughing at something. It must have been pretty funny because when Dal looked at the picture, he had to smile, too. His dad looked younger than his friends' dads, younger than Mr. Sabatini. That's because he stayed the same age, while everybody else kept getting older. The photograph was the last one taken of him while he was still on this earth.

Dal tried to think about something else. Thinking about death seemed like it might bring bad luck, but once you got started, how could you keep the thoughts from coming?

He said a quick prayer: "Dear God, please don't let me or anybody I know die. Not Mom or Grandma Rose or Mr. Sabatini or Kate. Or the Fosters, or any of the Puckets, especially not Patty Pucket." (He didn't want God to think he was selfish, just thinking of himself all the time.) "Say hi to my dad for me. Amen," he mouthed, letting out a long breath.

When he opened his eyes, Mrs. Pucket was rocking in her metal rocking chair, looking up at the trees.

When he had drunk his third glass of lemonade and chewed up all the ice, Dal got up from the lawn chair—you had to put your feet out sideways, holding on to the wooden supports, and walk away like a crab. He thanked Mrs. Pucket very much and said he was going to lie down for a while because he felt like he was starting to get a headache, which was a complete lie, but he didn't know how else to get away.

"That's a good idea," she said, getting up. "Think I will, too."

Unit Number 4 was hot. If you stayed in there for more than about a minute, you really would get a headache. Dal stayed just long enough to get some money out of his secret hiding place. Then, making sure no one was watching, he slipped out the door and locked it behind him. With the key in his pocket, he felt like a big kid who could come and go as he pleased. As he walked along the front of the motel and out into the street, he imagined that someone was watching him, even though no one was—he turned around to make sure. Maybe one of his friends back home was watching him on a spyscope. Detroit was very far away. He walked for eight blocks in a town nobody in Detroit had ever heard of. Why was Eden always so empty? *Because it had been attacked by the Russians, that's why. Now that they knew the secret formula, they had built an atom bomb and dropped it on America, and he was the only survivor. An old, beat-up pickup truck rumbled past. The driver was wearing a farmer's hat, but Dal could tell he was an enemy robot.*

Dal pulled the brim of his cowboy hat down over his eyes so the sun wouldn't blind him. In the window he was passing, he looked a little like Brandon de Wilde, the boy movie star. *There just happened to be a Hollywood producer in the shiny Buick coming toward him. He was out scouting locations for his next blockbuster film. He pulled over when he saw the boy in the cowboy hat, perfect for the lead. What's the movie going to be called? Dal asked, his hand on the rolled-down window. Little Britches. We want you for young Ralph Moody.*

Behind the bright reflection, the waitress from last night was waving at him. Dal wondered how long she had been watching. He hoped she didn't think he was conceited. He quickly waved and kept on going.

The movie theater was showing some lovey-dovey movie.

When he got to the Turners' store, he felt a momentary shyness—it was the first time he had gone in there by himself He straightened his shoulders and went in anyway, said hi to Mrs. Turner, who was busy at the counter, and marched to the back. They kept their Popsicles in a freezer that was big enough to put a dead body in. (*"We found him in there. He must have leaned in to get a Popsicle, and the door fell shut. It's a tragedy. I never should have left him alone at the motel all day," his grief-stricken "dad" stated.*) His feet off the ground, he unstuck a pair of Siamese Fudgsicles and took one up to the counter, where he also bought a pack of Juicy Fruit, a fire ball, and some sunflower seeds, so he'd have something to spit.

"You're Harry Sabatini's boy," Mrs. Turner said, ringing up the sale. It came to twenty-seven cents. "I didn't recognize you at first. How are you two doing? You have one heck of a nice stepdad—I guess you know that. You tell him I said hi."

Dal wanted to be friendly like his "nice" stepdad. He wanted to say in a loud voice, "I sure will, Mrs. Turner. Bye now!" Instead he mumbled, "Thanks." And added, "Don't I get any Green Stamps?"

She acted like she'd forgotten and gave him three. Should he have asked or not?

Going back outside was a shock. Heat came up from the asphalt in waves. No sooner had he tugged the wrapper off the Fudgsicle than it began dripping on his hand. He had to quick hold it over his tongue. He wished he had gotten two, but he didn't feel like going back in there.

The afternoon was lasting forever. It wasn't even two yet. He held on to the Fudgsicle stick because he didn't want to be a litterbug. When he got back to the motel, he broke the stick in half and dropped both pieces in the irrigation ditch that flowed along the street and into a culvert. He was the bigger half. If it won, his step-sister, Kate, would be okay, but if the little half came out first, she would have to be executed in the electric chair. He ran on the grass alongside the ditch, but the sticks disappeared into another culvert, and *neither* came out.

He could still save her, if he could hit the telephone pole with a stone in one throw, but he held on to the stone too long, and it bounced off the ground a few feet in front of him. Poor Kate. She was strapped to the electric chair and would die a miserable death unless the President pardoned her at the last minute. But unfortunately it wasn't the President. It was a Communist dictator from behind the Iron Curtain. He said Dal could have one more chance, and not wanting to see his stepsister fry, Dal got as close as he could to the telephone pole and threw underhand. The stone hit the pole. Whew.

Back home Kate probably didn't realize that her life had been spared.

The motel room was full of hot, tired air. He got his book and lay on his back to read some more.

A VISITOR

Somebody was pounding on the outside door. "Oh," he said, going to unlock it. He hated the way he felt after an afternoon nap. Like a zombie.

It was Mr. Sabatini. "Good meeting. Got a lot accomplished. I'm going to take a shower. It's ninety-six degrees in the shade out there." From the bathroom he called out, "So what did you do all day?"

Dal was sitting at the table with his head propped on his arm. His stepfather hadn't noticed the book. "Nothing," he said. His stepfather couldn't hear. *"Nothing!"* he shouted.

"Oh," Mr. Sabatini's voice said over the shower water. Then: "I have a surprise for you. Go over to Mrs. Pucket's. She's expecting you. What?"

"Do I have to?"

"I told her you'd be right over."

Dal closed the door to Unit Number 4 behind him. If it was ninety-six in the shade, it must be at least a hundred in the sun. Wanting to make sure that Mrs. Pucket heard him, Dal banged on the screen door, which rattled against the jamb. The person who appeared in the entryway was too short to be Mrs. Pucket.

"Patty!"

"Hey," she said, opening the door and coming out.

"What are you doing here?"

"Visiting my mamaw. I hitched a ride with your dad."

She was wearing a green-and-white checked shirt and Bermuda shorts and sandals. Her toenails were painted bright red.

"Show me where you live," she said.

Dal could hardly believe it was really and truly her. He had practically given up on ever seeing her again. She looked at him all set to smile if he said anything remotely funny, but his mind was a blank.

Half a minute later she was standing in their motel room. Dal felt weird. His stepfather's empty pants were on the davenport. So were his tired old boxer shorts. His stepfather himself was just getting out of the shower.

"Patty's here!" Dal called out quickly.

"Hello, Patty," Mr. Sabatini said through the closed door.

"Hello, Mr. Sabatini," Patty said back, grinning.

Brother. "You want to play catch? *We're going to be outside playing catch!"*

"Okay. I'll whistle when it's time for supper."

"Can Patty eat with us? You want to?"

"We're all eating at Mamaw's."

Nobody ever told him anything.

Patty held the ball up by her shoulder and flung it wildly. Dal didn't want to be a know-it-all and tell her she should wind up more and throw with her whole body. She could catch pretty well, though, but that was because Dal had given her his only glove. It looked huge on her skinny arm. Also, Dal was facing the setting sun, so it was harder to see the ball coming. It was embarrassing when he missed an easy throw, but he didn't want to make excuses.

One of her throws boinked off the green Hudson with Idaho plates that was always parked in front of Unit Number 1 in the late afternoon. The ball rolled across the grass and plopped into the irrigation ditch, where it bobbed like an apple. Dal fished it out before it went into the culvert. They stood there for a while, expecting the owner of the Hudson to come out and shout at them, but the door stayed shut, the blinds drawn.

"We better play somewhere else," Dal said.

"I know where," Patty said, leading the way. In back of the motel was a big field where you could tell cows had been (cow pies). A salt lick stood on the ground like a block of green ice. Patty squatted down and licked it, so Dal did, too. He had never tasted anything so salty.

Dal kicked a dry cow pie and kicked it again. "That's home plate." He tested a stick by whacking it on the ground. "You can bat first if you want to." He ran backward and stood by another cow pie. "This is the pitcher's mound. Anything to the right of that tree is an automatic out. So is anything to the left of the salt lick. Let's say you get only one out, since there's only two of us. If you get a hit, you have to run to the pitcher's mound and back again. That's a run. Otherwise, you have a man on first, and you get to be up again."

Patty said okay to all his rules. From the way she held the stick—off to one side—he figured she was an easy out. Then he would be up and nonchalantly hit the ball good-bye. He threw underhand, to make it easier for her, but he shouldn't have because at the last minute she reached back, swung the stick with all her might: *Whack!* The ball sailed over his head. He was running backward as fast as he could when his foot slid through a fresh cow pie and he ended up on his knees, praying. He scrambled to his feet again and ran to where the ball had last been seen, but what he thought was the ball, glowing in the weeds, turned out to be a white stone.

As he stood with his hands on his hips, trying to estimate how far the ball could have rolled, Patty was running back and forth between first base and home plate. "Seven," she called out. "Eleven . . . sixteen."

It was hopeless; the ball had been swallowed up by the earth.

"You won," Dal said philosophically. He didn't even raise his voice, which had a catch in it. Patty, still carrying the stick, loped past the pitcher's mound into the outfield, where Dal was walking in circles. From far away came Mr. Sabatini's whistle, which Dal had heard over the years calling Kate to supper: *wheet, whoo, whoo, whoo!* "We have to go now," he said gloomily. "I'll look for it tomorrow."

"I'm sorry," said Patty. "I didn't mean to hit it so hard."

Oh, boy. He felt squishy inside. When he trusted his voice, he said, "That's okay. You're a good hitter."

"You would have gotten me out easy, if the weeds hadn't've been so tall."

He felt like saying, "Shut up." Instead he took a deep breath. "Anyway, you won. How many runs did you get?"

"Only fifteen because my foot didn't really touch home plate one of the times." She grabbed hold of her ankle and raised her sandal as close to her face as she could and wrinkled her nose. "Do I have cow doo on me?" She danced on one foot, holding the other out for Dal to inspect.

"No, it's me. I slid through a pie."

Patty walked beside him. He knew she knew he felt bad, which only made it worse. The sky was getting dark. "You never got a chance to bat. Next time you'll be up first."

Between clenched teeth he said, "First, I have to get you out."

"Oh, that'll be easy," Patty said. "You'll probably get a hundred runs."

Mr. Sabatini's whistle filled the air, more impatient this time. Dal tried to whistle back, to signal they were coming. He could sort of whistle, but not very loud. He and Patty started jogging. At first they were just jogging home to supper; then Dal started racing in earnest. He ran with all his might to get to the wooden fence first, and huffing and puffing, his hands on his knees, he waited for Patty to catch up.

Mr. Foster and Len Pucket were sitting in metal chairs with Dal's stepfather, talking about something serious from the looks of them. The men paused long enough to say hi to Dal and Patty. Supper was hot dogs and potato chips and corn on the cob. Dal ate two hot dogs and three ears of corn, which for some reason pleased Mrs. Pucket. "I can put another hot dog on," she said.

"No thanks."

She dangled an unhusked ear in front of his face. "Want some more corn, hon? There's plenty."

Dal shook his head. He put his hand on his stomach and said in a loud voice that he was *"full!"* Patty had lime bug juice; Dal drank a glass of milk and licked his upper lip so he wouldn't have a mustache. For dessert they took turns churning strawberry ice cream in a bucket. But even before it was ready, Patty kicked his foot and frowned at him. When he still didn't get it, she jerked her head toward Main Street. In his ear she whispered, "Let's get out of here."

AT THE MOVIES

Dal whispered in Mr. Sabatini's ear: "Can me and Patty go some-where?" He didn't want the other grown-ups to hear. Mrs. Pucket had gotten up to go inside. The sign by her door came on. The OFF was pink and the ICE was orange. Bugs spun around the neon letters or crawled up the wood. Overhead the apricot trees were black, even the leaves.

Mr. Sabatini looked at Dal. "The ice cream's almost ready. Don't you want some ice cream?"

Dal looked at Patty. "Can we have ours later?"

"Well, where you off to?"

"You want to go to a movie?" Dal asked Patty.

"Sure."

Mrs. Pucket was coming through the door, carrying a stack of glass bowls. Even though she was supposed to be hard-of-hearing, she said, "Now you stay out of trouble, Patty Lynn Pucket!"

"Yes, ma'am," said Patty.

Mr. Sabatini glanced at the other men and then winked at Dal, but all he said was: "Be home by ten."

Dal and Patty stood under the lighted movie marquee that said AIR CONDITIONED FOR YOUR VIEWING COMFORT. "Look," said Patty, standing in front of one of the stills. "Clark Gable. He's sooo handsome."

His mom thought so, too. Dal couldn't figure it out. If you asked him, men with mustaches looked conceited, but he kept his opinion to himself.

He had never heard of the lady star. She wore too much makeup, and her eyelashes looked fake—but she had a big bosom. Men liked big bosoms, the bigger the better, though why Dal sure didn't know.

"Come on," Patty said, yanking him by the hand.

The girl in the booth was a teenager. She wore a pink sweater even in this hot weather and pointy black glasses, and she was reading a love comic. Patty knew her. "Hey, Wilhelmina," she said.

Wilhelmina opened the little window. "Hey, Patty. You going to want something to eat?"

Patty looked at Dal. "Popcorn," he said, so Patty nodded.

Wilhelmina leaned forward to make sure no one else was coming. Then she shut the little window, got up from her stool, opened a door in the back of the booth, and when Dal and Patty went inside, she stood waiting to tear their ticket. It was too cold in the theater. Dal's arms had goose bumps. He wished he had worn his sweatshirt. Wilhelmina had gone behind the candy counter and was bending over. At the flick of a switch the popcorn popper lit up. She made a flattened box into the right shape and used it to scoop up the popcorn. "That'll be ten cents," she said. Dal paid for everything with his own money. In a loud whisper she added, "Enjoy the movie."

"We will," said Patty. But it was so boring Dal could hardly sit still. He threaded his arms inside his T-shirt to keep from freezing. They had missed the first part of the show, but you could sort of figure out what it was about. The lady liked Clark Gable, but for some reason she pretended not to. When he tried to kiss her, she reached back and slapped him with all her might.

With his chin in the collar of his T-shirt, Dal looked at Patty to see how she was taking it. She flinched.

There were only seven people in the movie theater besides them. A man came in and stood in the back for a while. He walked down the aisle slowly and sat down next to Dal, even though there were about a hundred free seats.

"Hey, buddy," he whispered, "want some Milk Duds?"

Dal's heart was beating. He felt like he couldn't breathe. He pretended he hadn't heard, but the man tapped him on the chest with his box of candy.

"Want some of my Milk Duds?"

Dal looked at him for a billionth of a second. "No thanks." Even the man's sweat smelled of whiskey.

Like a ventriloquist, without moving his lips, he said to Patty, "Want to move?" She bent forward to look at the man and nodded.

They nonchalantly stood up and walked to the front row, where there was an aisle on one side and a broken seat on the other. Without turning his head, Dal could see the man get up and start down the far aisle. Patty had her eye on him, too.

"That's Roy Ammons," she said. "They won't let him go near his own children."

Luckily he sat down next to some other people.

Dal leaned his head way back and looked at the giant screen. Clark Gable's goggly eyes were the size of baseballs. The lady's bosom was bigger than Dal. The popcorn box was empty, so he tore pieces off and flicked them at Patty, who didn't even notice, she was so enraptured by the movie.

Finally he couldn't stand it anymore. He leaned over and said, "You like this movie?"

She turned her shining eyes on him. "Why," she said, "don't you?"

"I think it's junk."

"We can go if you want to."

"Well, not if you're enjoying it."

"We don't have to stay."

"It's not that bad, I guess."

After a minute she said, "Come on." They ducked down so their heads wouldn't be silhouetted on the screen. But it didn't matter. Everybody else was slouched in the seats, probably smooching. They raced up the aisle and through the padded doors. Wilhelmina was talking to a teenage boy who looked like a hood. His hair was slicked back, and he had sideburns.

"So long, Patty," she said, leaning around the boy.

Outside, it was raining. They stopped under the awning of a dry-goods store so Patty could ooh and aah over a skirt in the window.

"Isn't it cute?"

Dal looked. It was green. How should he know? He hated it when girls treated him like one of their girlfriends.

"You didn't like the movie?" she said as they continued walking along in the rain. It wasn't coming down that hard. "It was so sad because they came from different backgrounds, and now he was going away, and they would probably never see each other again."

Was that what it was about? How come she knew and he didn't? Were girls really smarter than boys about stupid things like movies and books?

"I think it stunk, if you want to know my honest opinion."

"Why?"

He didn't want to have to say why because he didn't know why; it just did. "Because it was so fake," he said finally, and spit.

"Clark Gable, though. He's a dreamboat. And what's-her-name? She's gorgeous."

Dal stopped and just looked at her.

"What?"

"You're a hundred times cuter than her."

Patty's whole body tightened up. She looked off in space. Then she said softly, "Thanks for the compliment."

Oh, boy. He hadn't meant to compliment her. He was just stating a fact of nature.

They stood under the Two Spud sign, which gave them little or no protection from the rain. Drops boinked off the lights. If they kept going, they'd be back at the motel in about two minutes. Somewhere over the desert thunder crashed.

"Come on," said Patty, starting up a side street. Dal ran after her. If he tried to kiss her, would she slap him? Why did girls slap?

They ran under trees, noisy with rain, past empty-looking houses. Mr. Sabatini had said that they were tearing down the old elementary school because the population of Eden was dwindling. The school's front doors were all boarded up.

"I went there," said Patty, pointing with her wet face. Her hair was all stringy. He followed her around to the other side. Somebody had propped a board against a windowsill—like the gangplank to an ark. Patty crawled up on her hands and feet like a cat and disappeared inside. There was no sign that said you couldn't trespass. Dal stepped cautiously on the board. He held his hands out for balance. He ended up on the windowsill and jumped in.

They were in a classroom with rows of desks all covered with plaster. Each desk had a hole in the corner for an inkwell. A framed picture of Abraham Lincoln hung on the wall. Old Abe looked like he was resting his beard on his shirtfront.

"You're late, Dal Wilkins," Patty said. She was sitting at the teacher's desk.

Dal quickly took a seat. He said, "The front door was locked."

"That's no excuse. If you do one more bad thing, I will have to paddle you."

Oh, brother, Dal thought.

"Now, class." She stood up and came around to the front of the desk. She had a wooden pointer in her hands. "Take out your books and turn to page one hundred thirty-seven. Dal?"

"I don't have a book. I must have left it at home."

Patty was standing right next to him, hitting the pointer against the palm of one hand. She looked like a wet cat. "Let's see if you've done your homework. What's the capital of Maryland?"

"Mary?"

"Ha-ha, very funny. Who is the President of the United States?"

"Wait, I know that one. Howdy Doody!"

She was shaking her head.

"When was the Civil War?"

"Holy cow, how should I know? A long time ago. A hundred years."

"Wrong, 1861 to 1865." She pulled his ear (hard, too).

"Ow!"

In a tired voice she said, "Go to the board, please, Dal Wilkins."

He went to the board. In the little gutter thing was a piece of chalk.

"This is your last chance. I'm rooting for you, son. What is one thousand one hundred sixty-six divided by three hundred twenty-two?" She looked at her empty wrist. "You have exactly three minutes. Go!"

Three hundred twenty-two divided into 1,166? That was easy; he could do it in his head. Three times 322 equaled 966. 1,166 take away 966 equaled 200 and not quite two thirds. Rounding off, he wrote a big "3.6" and, next to it, drew a picture of a head with spaghetti hair and crossed eyes. Its tongue was hanging out. Underneath he wrote, "Miss Pucket."

When he turned around, Patty was sitting at one of the desks with her head propped up in her hands, watching him.

"Miss Patty Pucket," said Dal, boosting himself up onto the teacher's desk. "Is that how we sit in the sixth grade?"

Patty quickly straightened up and folded her hands neatly on the table in front of her. "No, sir."

"That's better. I don't want to have to paddle you. Now, class, let's find out something about Patty, shall we? When were you born?"

"October 22, 1941."

"What is your mother's name?"

"Trudy Akitt."

"Your father's?"

"My real father is Leonard Pucket. My stepfather is C. J. McAdoo, only I hate his guts."

Dal froze. You could tell from her fierce look that she wasn't kidding. He wanted to ask Patty *why* she hated C. J. McAdoo's guts, but he didn't dare. Sometimes he and Mr. Sabatini didn't see eye to eye, but he didn't hate his guts.

He waited a few seconds, and then, as if she hadn't said anything out of the ordinary, he went on. "Now go to the board, please, Patty Pucket, and write out the twelve times table."

Patty slipped out of her desk and walked primly to the front of the room. She set the pointer down on the desk, picked up a piece of chalk, and drew a big heart with an arrow through it. Dal's heart was going crazy. Inside the heart, she wrote, "P. P. + ?" Suddenly Dal felt tired and weak. "Who?" he said. She smiled at him, tilting her face sideways. "That's for me to know and you to find out."

He hated it when girls said things like that.

In that instant everything turned black and white, like on television. Three seconds later—*Idaho one and Idaho two and Idaho three and*—thunder banged right overhead. They both jumped. A siren started going, *waaaoh, waaoh, waaoh.*

"Air-raid drill," said Dal.

Patty walked calmly to the nearest desk, climbed underneath, and folded her arms over her head.

"Is that what you do in an air-raid drill?"

"Why? What do you all do?"

"If it was a real atomic bomb, your skin would come off like a cooked chicken."

Patty slid out from under the desk and leaned back on her outstretched arms.

"Maybe it would protect you from broken glass. In my school we form a long line, walk quietly down the hallway and down the basement. Only that's really dumb, too. If there really was a bomb, the boiler would explode, and we'd all be scalded to death."

"Don't talk about it. It gives me nightmares."

"Me and my friend Jimmy always stand at the beginning of the line so we get to go down the basement first. The stairs are metal. You can look through them." When she still didn't get it, he said, "You can look up girls' skirts."

Patty stared at him hard for a second. "Boys have filthy minds," she said.

Dal tried to smile, but his smile felt crooked on his face, like he hadn't put it on right. Why had he told her that? *She* was a girl.

Boys did have filthy minds, it was true.

Just then a man's voice said something right outside the window. The end of the plank wobbled.

Dal and Patty dashed out in the hallway and into the first room they came to. It was a bathroom, only it didn't have any urinals.

His heart was racing. The room was dark, the windows looked like gray gaping holes. Patty took long, sliding steps away from him. "In here," she called in a whisper. Dal felt his way along the sinks and into the stall where Patty was. She quickly shut the door.

"They better not come in here," her hot breath said in his ear. "It's for girls only."

"Who is it?"

"I don't know, but it might be that creep Roy Ammons."

They listened for a while. It sounded like someone was breaking glass.

"What would he do if he found us?"

"Something real creepy."

Holding on to a pipe that came down from the ceiling, Patty climbed up on the toilet seat. She gave him her hand, and he climbed up facing her. The seat was wobbly, but they stood still for about a whole minute, holding their breaths. The intruder might be opening the door to the bathroom very quietly, though all Dal could hear was water gurgling overhead and Patty breathing through her mouth. Their chests were touching. It felt like they had one heart between them—and it was going berserk.

Dal had never been in a girls' bathroom before. It felt even weirder to be in there with a girl.

Finally he couldn't stand it anymore and got down. He quietly opened the door to the stall. There was no one there. He crossed the bathroom and opened the door to the hallway, listening with all his might. After a while he said in his regular voice, "It's okay. They're gone. You can come out now."

"Wait," said Patty through the shut door.

When she came out, he pretended he hadn't heard anything. "The flusher's broke," she said, tucking her shirt in.

It was still raining out. Some drops splashed in through the broken windows.

"Now where are you going?" Dal asked in a panic.

Patty was pushing the door marked "Boys." "You can't go in there," he said. He went in after her.

"You went in the girls' room," Patty said. "I want to see what it looks like."

Dal was aghast. "There's nothing to see," he said, looking around. The boys' stalls didn't have doors on them. They didn't at his school, either. It wasn't fair. If you had to poop, everyone could see. Patty stood on her tiptoes in front of one of the urinals that seemed to glow in the dark, holding the front of her shorts. She went *pssss*. She was laughing, but he sure wasn't. "Is that how you do it?"

"I'm getting out of here," Dal said. His ears were burning.

"Wait," said Patty. She pulled the flusher, and the urinal made a hissing noise like a snake, but no water came out.

They ran out into the hall and back to the first room. Somebody had been smoking a cigarette in there. Dal went to the window. The board was gone. "Now how are we going to get out? We'll have to jump."

"Look," said Patty. "That's disgusting." Somebody had added breasts to the picture of Miss Pucket. She quickly erased it with the side of her hand.

A second siren wailed. Yikes! Dal was sitting on the windowsill. He rolled over onto his stomach, hung by his hands. It was still a long drop. "Dal!" Patty's face was in the window. He let go of one hand, swung loose, tried to see the ground. It came up hard. He was on all fours, his hands and knees soaked with mud. He jumped up and was lifting the board back in place when Patty dropped down beside him.

"You moron," he said. "You could have broken your leg."

"You could have, too, moron."

They ran back to Main Street. The rain was ending. The siren was gone.

"We're going to be in trouble," Dal said, looking at his watch. It was after ten-thirty.

"Why? We didn't do anything. You know, you don't have to be so good all the time."

URANIUM

The lights were off in Unit Number 4. "They're over at Len's," Patty said. She walked to the corner unit, Number 7, and went inside, letting the screen door rattle shut behind her. Dal lingered a minute in the semidark, looking in. Jerry Foster, Len Pucket, and his stepfather were all sitting at the kitchen table. Mr. Sabatini was holding an official-looking document with wavy colors on it. Old Mrs. Pucket sat in a rocking chair, sewing through a hoop of cloth. When Patty went over to her, she took her hand in both of hers.

Dal went inside, too. "What's going on?" he said to Patty in a low voice. On the table was a saucer full of salty peanuts. Patty was reaching for some. Dal took some, too.

Before Patty could answer, Len caught her. "Here's my sweet pea," he said, but Patty ducked out of his arms and went and stood by her grandmother again. She popped peanuts into her mouth one by one.

Dal went over to Mr. Sabatini and put his foot on the rung of his chair. His stepfather tilted his head back. "You may be looking at the biggest sucker in the world, Dal. I'm about to become a part owner of a uranium mine."

Mr. Foster said, "Maybe we should let the boy hear. See what he thinks."

Len Pucket watched them with a smile on his face, but you couldn't tell what he was thinking. It was like the real Len was sitting behind the smile, looking out, and you couldn't see the expression on *his* face. "Son," he said, "how'd you like to make your daddy a rich man and help me out in the bargain?" The ash on his cigarette was half an inch long. He held it over a sardine can already full of butts but didn't tap it.

"How'd you like to spend the rest of your life in a motel room?" Patty piped up in a mocking voice.

Dal looked around. So this was where Patty's real father lived. Funny he hadn't seen him around the motel before. Unit Number 7 was identical to Unit Number 4, except there was a lot more junk piled up in it.

Len Pucket didn't get mad at Patty for her smart-alecky remark. He took a long puff on his cigarette, lifted his lips, and blew smoke at the ceiling. The ash was practically an inch long now, and it still didn't fall off. "If you was rich, you could buy yourself a brand-new TV with an eight-inch screen and watch all your favorite shows. You could buy your mommy something nice, a purdy necklace or diamond earrings."

"Knowing her, she'd rather have something practical, like a washing machine," Mr. Sabatini put in, "but go on."

Dal was on mental high alert. "What would I have to do?" he asked.

"Who-ah! I knew it. That boy's nobody's fool. Now, listen, son, and try to understand, because this is complicated, but it's real important. I own some land down near the Utah border in a place called Rattler's Gulch. It used to have a silver mine on it, which I owned fifty percent of. My partner and I made a lot of money off that mine. Oh, I know it don't look like it now. But your daddy can tell you if there's a word I say that isn't true."

His "daddy" sat there, not saying anything one way or the other. Dal couldn't keep from staring at the ash on the end of Len Pucket's cigarette.

"Now this mine I'm telling you about, my ex-partner and I took every dollar's worth of silver out of that hole in the ground. Then, bless his soul, he sold me his share of what he and everybody else figured was a worthless piece of rattlesnake-infested no-man's-land for one thousand bucks. He laughed when he pocketed my check, which didn't bother me none—I been worse than laughed at. He said, 'Len, there ain't enough silver ore left in that hole to smelt a ring for a baby's little finger, and you shoulda known better.' I thanked him kindly, like he was tellin' me something I didn't already know, and waited till I was in my truck to start chucklin', because see, I'd been back to our diggings with my Geiger counter. You seen for yourself how it started squawking soon as I put those specimens up to it?"

Here Len Pucket began impersonating a Geiger counter, clicking his teeth and shaking his head like a jack-in-the-box. Ash sprinkled down on everything. He started swatting at the front of his fancy shirt. Everyone laughed, even Patty, who looked long-legged, half sitting in Mrs. Pucket's lap.

When things quieted down, Len said in a solemn voice, "Son, that old silver mine turns out to have one of the biggest deposits of uranium ore that has been found in the United States to the present time. I can't explain it. It may be *co-in-ci-dence;* it may be *fate.* I personally own one hundred and forty acres—that's the mine, the scrubland on all sides, and the mineral rights all the way to China. So what am I telling you all this for? I'm sitting on a uranium mine!" he said, springing up, as if something had gone off under him.

Patty was all the way in old Mrs. Pucket's lap now, her feet just barely touching the floor. Dal noticed that whenever Len Pucket said something funny, he glanced over at Patty to see her reaction. Patty was laughing so hard you could see her gums.

"But you can see for yourself"—he raised his hands to the motel walls—"*I* ain't got no money. And I need money—lots of it—to clear the land, lay in a road so that trucks can move freely to the mine site and back out again. I need a processing hut, I need water, I need dynamite, I need gasoline. This ain't no two-man, pick-and-shovel operation. If I could run it by myself, I guess I would, but I know it's better to be wise than greedy. Besides, there's enough uranium in there to make twenty men rich. Maybe more."

"Exactly how much *do* you need?" Jerry Foster asked.

"Ten thousand dollars to start operations. The Pentagon offered to buy me out and then turn around and make me foreman. I may look dumb, but I ain't; I turned them down. Once we're up and running, the Pentagon will be back with every vehicle at their disposal. By then the mine will be paying for itself, that I guarantee. Dividends could go as high as a two hundred percent return on investment, and that's being conservative."

"How much would it cost?" Dal asked. He looked to see if Patty had heard him.

"I'm selling blocks of a hundred shares minimum for a hundred dollars. That's a lot of money, I know, but keep in mind that this is uranium we're talking about. Now that them Rosenbergs gave away our secret formula to the Russkies, there's nothing stopping them from making their own atom bombs. They'll build them one, we'll build us one, they'll build a thousand, we'll do the same thing, until both sides of the Iron Curtain is armed with enough deadly weapons to end civilization as we know it. In every one of them bombs the main ingredient is . . . *u-ran-i-um.*" He put his elbows on the table. He was talking directly to Dal. "But that ain't all," he said. "This ain't just about bombs and blowing mankind off the face of the earth. You're going to be a scientist someday, am I right?"

"Maybe," said Dal with his arms crossed.

"Well, you know that the atom is a hundred times more powerful than coal or gasoline or any other fuel known to man. It has the capability to provide heat and electricity for whole cities. By the time you're old enough to get behind the wheel of a car, people will be driving atomic automobiles. I hope you can imagine that because I sure can't. Instead of going to the gas station and fillin' up the old buggy with gas, I reckon you'll just pop a stone from our mine into the atom tank and she'll run for a year, maybe more."

Mr. Foster had taken out his billfold. He was counting money into a pile. Each bill was new and crisp and had a picture of Alexander Hamilton on it. "Heck," he said, grinning sheepishly, "I'm a gambling man."

From her grandmother's lap, where she had somehow found room to sprawl, Patty said, "Margaret is going to kill you."

"Not if we don't tell her, she's not. Not if we let it be a surprise."

There was a brief silence: *uranium one, uranium two.* Dal felt like everyone was watching him, waiting to hear what he would say. If he said, "I don't think we can afford it," would Len Pucket get mad?

Mr. Pucket had a coughing fit. He stood up and went over to the sink to spit. When he came back, he said in a low voice, "Can I have a word with you outside?" Dal looked at Mr. Sabatini, who shrugged his shoulders.

"Don't believe a word he says," Patty called after Dal as he and Len stepped out into the quiet courtyard and shut the door behind him. The air smelled clean, now that the rain had ended. Mr. Pucket bowed away from Dal to light a cigarette, casting a giant shadow on the side of the motel. He sucked the smoke in through his mouth and nose. Then, without saying anything, the two of them walked the length of courtyard and out into the street. Invisible water gurgled in the irrigation ditch.

Mr. Pucket hunched his shoulders like it was cold out, but it wasn't—it was mild. He spit a couple of times, and then he chuckled—unhappily, it seemed to Dal.

"Not believe your own daddy," Len Pucket said, shaking his head. "You ever hear anything like that? But I got it coming to me, that and more. I let a lot of people down, drinking and gambling. There ain't nobody more sorry or ashamed than I am. But the good Lord seen fit to give me another chance. I ain't played cards for more than pennies in over two years. And I've been dry for going on eighteen months. Them are facts."

Dal was embarrassed.

"You like her, don't you?" said Len Pucket, looking at him for about half a second. "I know you do, and I'm glad. See, I don't care nothing about making money for myself anymore. The things I need don't cost much, and the things I want money can't buy. But if I did have some money, and if I stay like I'm going, sober and dry, I might could, you know, make her so she's proud of me. You understand what I'm saying, son?"

Dal nodded his head hard. "I have forty dollars in my room. Should I go get it?"

"I wouldn't let you if I didn't think it was in your own best interest. You believe that, don't you?"

"Y-yes," said Dal.

Len Pucket put his cigarette in his mouth and shook Dal's hand with both of his. "It looks like we're in this together, partner."

Dal's money was in his straw-colored suitcase, under his bed. Twenty dollars he had earned; the other twenty dollars his mom had given him for the trip. When he got back to Unit Number 7, everybody watched as he counted the money onto the table.

"You sure you want to do this?" Mr. Sabatini said.

Dal nodded. "I'm sure."

Mr. Sabatini wrote out a check for the remainder and handed it to Len Pucket, who didn't look at it but bowed his head. Then the men and Dal stood up and solemnly shook each other's hands. I own a uranium mine, Dal thought. Well, part of one. He wondered if their share of the profits would arrive in the form of a check or as a thick wad of bills. *It's money, his mom would say, opening the envelope. A lot of it, too. I wonder where it came from?*

Patty came up and shook his hand, too. "Sucker!" she said.

"When are you planning on starting up operations?" Mr. Foster asked Len.

"It won't be long now. Al Spivey and his boys have to build me a road first."

"When do you figure on bringing up the first uranium?"

"I'm learning the business as I go. Before the year is out is as near as I can guess. But I'm here, I'll be in touch, you'll be closely informed."

A year! Already Dal was beginning to have doubts.

"Come on," Mr. Sabatini said, his hand on Dal's shoulder. "We've gambled away enough money for one night."

Mrs. Pucket stood up, on the third try.

Mr. Foster said, "Come on, Patty. I'll take you home."

"Bye, Patty."

"Bye, Dal."

CHAPTER 13

THE DUNNS

Mr. Dunn didn't say much except "yep," so Mr. Sabatini had to do most of the talking. "This is my boy I was telling you about. He has his heart set on doing some horseback riding, but he's strictly a beginner. I don't think you've ever been on a horse, have you, Dal?"

Dal had a ringing sound in his ears. Sometimes Mr. Sabatini had about as much sense as an American buffalo. *Yes,* he had been horseback riding before—and Mr. Sabatini had been there, too!

"I rode a horse that time at Belle Isle," Dal said through his teeth. "At your company's picnic, remember?" Grr. He had ridden pretty well, too, for someone who had never been on a horse before. Only the animal they gave him, a mare, had a mind of her own. She wandered along the path last in line. The moment the others disappeared around a bend, she lowered her head, shaking it from side to side to free herself from the reins, and started nibbling grass. No amount of yanking on the reins or muttering "giddyup" would induce her to begin walking again. In desperation Dal had dug the heels of his gym shoes into her flanks. The mare's large head with eyes the size of eggs swung around to look at him. That was enough to persuade Dal to let the reins hang freely and wait for the riding instructor to rescue him.

"You've got horses," Mr. Sabatini was saying in the voice he reserved for people he didn't think were too bright.

Mr. Dunn chuckled into his shirtfront. "That's a fact," he said, not looking at either Mr. Sabatini or Dal. "We do have horses."

As the three of them were standing in the yard, talking, a large boy came out of the house, followed by two younger kids, a girl who kept smiling at Dal with her head tilted to the side and an unsmiling boy of seven or eight. The large boy, fully a head taller than Dal, wiped his mouth on the length of his flannel shirtsleeve and grinned. Dal's heart sank. If this was Mr. Dunn's boy, he doubted that he could ever be friends with him. He looked a little like Larry Wiedenhof, plus he had teeth that were like giant kernels of corn with a space between the front two.

"You must be Wilbur," Mr. Sabatini said in his friendliest voice. "This is Dal."

Dal shook Wilbur's hand, but the other boy didn't squeeze back the way you're supposed to. Bro-ther! How come nothing ever turns out the way you plan?

Meanwhile, the boy's sister came up to Dal and held out her hand, too. "I'm Melissa," she said, "only you can call me Missy. Everybody does. Are you going to stay with us? Because if you are, you're going to have to sleep in *his* bed." She pointed to her other brother, the serious-looking one. "He's Joe Ed." When his name was mentioned, Joe Ed stepped forward and shook Dal's hand, too. He had a hard grip for so young a boy. Missy said, "Joe Ed's going to have to sleep with me. I don't mind, only Joe Ed poots." She put her hand over her mouth and opened her eyes wide.

Dal looked at the three of them in amazement.

Wilbur cuffed his sister with his big hand and said, "Get back in the house, Missy, and finish your breakfast. Don't be telling tales."

When his stepfather caught Dal's eye, he beckoned for him to follow him over to the pickup. "I've got to get going," he said in a low voice, his foot on the running board. "The Dunns have very kindly offered to put you up until Friday, *if* you want to stay. Or you can come with me—I have to drive out to Burley to see a farmer. It's entirely up to you." He squinted at Dal like he was trying to read his mind.

Dal didn't know what to say. He sure as heck didn't feel like driving out to Burley to see a farmer. "I'll stay, I guess," he said, sighing.

"Good," Mr. Sabatini said. "Keep an open mind. You might enjoy yourself." He handed Dal the suitcase they had packed just in case and added in a low voice, "Next free weekend, maybe we'll drive down to the Utah border and take a look at our mine. How'd that be?"

He winked, and Dal couldn't help smiling.

As soon as Mr. Sabatini had driven away, leaving Dal alone with complete strangers, Mr. Dunn said to his son, "You better take him inside and feed him some breakfast. Be sure you get your chores done, mind. He can go along, if he wants, but he don't have to. He's our guest."

"Yes, sir," said Wilbur, grinning his toothy grin. To Dal he said, "Come on."

They went up some wooden stairs, through a screen door, into the kitchen. "Shut that door, Wilbur Dunn," shouted a fat woman, sitting at the table and feeding a baby in a high chair. She smiled sweetly at Dal, as though she hadn't just hollered at her son, and put another spoonful of white stuff into the baby's mouth. The baby jerked her hands up and down and tried to swat the spoon out of her mouth. As soon as the spoon was taken away, she let the white stuff dribble down her chin and glanced around to see who was watching.

It was stuffy in the kitchen with the door shut. The windows were shut, too. Dal's house was sometimes a mess if they weren't expecting company, but he had never seen anything like this dump. Dishes were stacked wherever there was any space—and there wasn't much. The patterned linoleum was curling up in several places; you could see the nailed floorboards underneath. The curtains drooping in the windows looked like they had been cut from old dresses. Maybe they're poor, Dal thought.

"Sit down," Mrs. Dunn said politely to Dal. "What do you usually have for your breakfast?"

Dal sat down, eyeing the table suspiciously. A giant box of corn-flakes stood open in front of him—that looked safe enough. But next to it was a glass pitcher full of pale white milk—straight from the cow, no doubt. You could see milk things floating on the surface.

"Actually I already had breakfast. Back at the motel. But thank you."

The baby clapped her hands and produced a bubble from her rosy lips.

As soon as they could get away from the breakfast table, Dal followed Wilbur back outside. They went around the barn, stooped to pass under an electric wire ("That'll give you a surprise"), and came to a pen full of enormous pigs. One thrust its snout against the chicken wire and grunted from deep inside its head. Wilbur kicked the fence with his heavy foot. "Get back, you stupid sow!" he shouted. Dal expected the pig to turn around and run off squealing, but it only jumped back on all four trotters and continued grunting. It watched them with its hard little eyes.

"Doesn't that hurt it?"

"That sow is so mean she would eat your foot if she got a chance. I ain't kidding, either."

Wilbur had lugged a bucket of leftovers from the kitchen. He lifted it over the fence and dumped it right on the ground. The baby's pabulum was on top, like tiny pearls. The pigs were so greedy, they shoveled the food right into the dirt and ate that, too. Dal kept his feet away from the big sow.

As he followed Wilbur to the barn, Dal said, "What grade are you in?"

"I got put back," Wilbur said matter-of-factly. "I have to do sixth grade over. I reckon it'll be easy the second time around. I hate school, don't you?"

"It's for the birds," Dal agreed.

"Our teacher, Miss Barnett?" said Wilbur. "She's as mean as that old sow. Fat, too. She can hardly get out the door. She has bosoms down to here." He laughed so hard, slobber appeared on his chin. To be polite, Dal laughed, too.

There was a man in the barn, hosing down the cement floor. He nodded at Dal but didn't smile or say anything. The barn was warm and smelled of living animals. It was noisy, too, with a motor running. About ten cows were lined up in a row, three with milking machines attached to their teats. They all looked around when the boys came in; one of them stepped loudly against the floor with her hard hooves and mooed. The man shouted something to Wilbur that Dal didn't get. "I'm going to," Wilbur said peevishly, patting one of the cows.

He put his mouth close to Dal's ear. "Want a drink?" he said. Without waiting for an answer, he squatted under the cow and pulled one of its teats practically to his lips. A stream of watery milk splashed in his open mouth. Scrambling out from underneath, he swished the milk from one cheek to the other, like he was rinsing his mouth. Then he spit it into a shallow moat that ran along the edge of the wall. He used his shirtsleeve from the elbow to the cuff to wipe his face.

"Want to try?"

Dal didn't really dislike Wilbur, he thought, getting down under the cow's belly, trying to avoid the powerful-looking legs. But he felt like he was going to have to act dumber than he was, the way he did around some of his friends at school, since he didn't want to show off. Dal was a city kid; Wilbur was a hick.

He wasn't sure what to do with the teat, now that he had his fist around it. The cow's warm belly was awfully close to his face, and he hadn't bothered to make friends with her first. She was probably thinking along the same lines—who was this strange boy?—because she eyed him around one of her forelegs. Her eye had the shine of alarm on it. Dal had never realized before how big a cow was. If her legs gave way, he was a pancake. She had a warm smell, sort of a mixture of pee and manure and milk. Her milk sac looked like an actual sack of milk, with white hairs growing on it. It also looked like it was about to burst. What would it be like to carry around so much weight all the time? Here goes, he thought, pulling on the teat as though it were a spigot in a soda shop. He got a face full of warm milk; some of it even went in his eye. The next thing he knew he was sitting in some dirt that probably wasn't dirt.

Wilbur cracked up. "City slicker," he said, dancing around like an idiot. "You have to aim. Open your mouth more wider."

Dal got into position again, opened his mouth as wide as he could, closed both eyes, and this time the milk went where it was supposed to—except that he didn't know what to do with it, so much warm milk that he had trumpeter's cheeks. Struggling to his feet, he spit where Wilbur had spit. He spit around ten times to get the raw taste out of his mouth. He also kept licking the inside of his mouth, to see what the taste was like. It was watery and almost sweet. The worst part was that it was warm. Dal hated even room-temperature milk.

Plus his butt was soaked through with—there was no mistaking it now—liquid cow manure.

As Dal was wiping his mouth on the back of his hand, the man suddenly appeared around the cow's flank. He glowered at Dal and raised his hand like he was going to hit Wilbur. Wilbur ducked. The man's mouth was full of something he was chewing, not gum. He spit a long, flying yellow puddle in the same place the boys had spit. Then, with his wad of tobacco tucked into one bulging cheek, he snarled something Dal couldn't understand.

"Yes, sir," Wilbur muttered. To Dal he said, "Let's get out of here."

"Who was that?" Dal asked as soon as they were back outside.

Wilbur said a swearword. "He works for my dad. His name is Faubus."

"Will we get into trouble? I'll say it was my fault, too."

"Forget it," Wilbur said. "He won't tell. If he does, I can tell a thing or two that I saw him do once." And he whispered something in Dal's ear that was so incredible that Dal promptly decided it couldn't be true.

"Where are the horses?" Dal asked nonchalantly as they walked back toward the house. Wilbur had said he wanted a "snack."

"My daddy has 'em over by the canyon."

"Want to go see? Maybe we can go horseback riding."

Wilbur grunted. "You can, if you want. You're the guest. I see 'em all the time."

"Do you have one of your own?" Dal asked.

"A horse? They belong to my daddy. I *been* on a horse before. Shoot, I've ridden just about every animal you can name. I been on a cow and a pig, and I even tried riding a chicken once and broke its neck."

Dal laughed.

"I ain't kiddin'," said Wilbur.

IN TROUBLE

Mrs. Dunn was sitting alone at the kitchen table, turning the pages of a movie magazine. "Wilbur," she said, "how many times have I told you not to mess with them cows?"

"Who said we were messing? Faubus? He's a dang liar. I was showing *him* around like you said."

"And I guess I just imagined it when I told you to mind your little brother and sister."

"We was doing chores!" Wilbur wailed. "I can't take them brats everywhere!"

In another room the baby started crying.

"Uh-huh. And now you gone and woke the baby. Well, you can go to your room for an hour, or I can tell your daddy when he comes home how you've been acting in front of our guest, and him and you can discuss it out in the barn. It's up to you."

Wilbur clenched both fists and shook them in the air. "It ain't fair," he whimpered, tears dripping down both cheeks.

Dal quickly said, "It was my fault, too, Mrs. Dunn. I asked him to show me how to milk a cow." The words *him and you can discuss it out in the barn* made him feel cold inside. He wondered if *he* would have to go out to the barn with Mr. Dunn. He wasn't sure what happened when you got there, but he could imagine.

Mrs. Dunn smiled at him sweetly. "You are our guest," she said. "You can go outside and have a rest if you want to. I'll tell them little kids to leave you alone. I bet it's different out here than where you live. You from Chicago?"

"Detroit," Dal said. "Michigan."

Wilbur said cheerfully, "That's where all our cars come from."

"The Motor City," Dal said, feeling like an advertisement.

Before he could think of anything else interesting to say about his hometown, Mrs. Dunn screamed, "Shut that door, Wilbur, or I'll kill you."

Wilbur slammed the refrigerator door, but not before he had grabbed something off one of the shelves. He held it behind his back, a box of Velveeta cheese.

His mother struggled up from the table—it wasn't easy because of her size—and went over to take the box of cheese away from her overgrown son. But Wilbur held it over his head.

"Give it," she said, holding out her hand.

"Uh-uh," said Wilbur, grinning.

"If I have an asthma attack," she said, starting to wheeze, "I'll—" She didn't finish her sentence, because a spasm of coughing seized her.

In the background the baby was screeching.

Wilbur was opening his prize when Mrs. Dunn took another swipe at it. She might have gotten it this time, if he hadn't seen her coming and jumped back just in time. "Ha-ha, missed me."

Mrs. Dunn backed into her chair, picked up her magazine, and used it to fan her face. "I bet *he* don't backtalk to his mama like that."

Dal felt like a newspaper reporter, spying on these people's lives. He wished they would call him by his name, instead of referring to him as the *guest* all the time. I should have gone with Mr. Sabatini to see that farmer, he thought.

"If I was you, I'd take my hour, unless I wanted to stay inside all day."

"Can we bring some food with us? Him and me are hungry."

"You can eat when it's time, same as everyone else. I'll call you."

"Come on," said Wilbur, dropping the cheese on the table.

"He can, if he wants, to keep you company, but he don't have to. *He* can have something to eat if he wants." She looked at Dal. "I could boil you an egg."

"No thanks," Dal said.

The baby's screaming reached its fiercest pitch, and then, mid-note, it stopped. The effort must have worn her out.

"That's where you're going to sleep," Wilbur said, pointing to an unmade bed. The blanket had mostly disappeared between the bed and the wall. His host plopped down on the other bed, retrieved a concave horror comic book from under the pillow, and began to read. "Be careful," he said as Dal went to sit down. "Joe Ed, he sometimes wets his bed."

Dal lifted the sheets. They looked dry. When he spent the night at Jimmy Beard's or vice versa, their mothers always changed the sheets. Cowboys slept in bunkhouses and didn't need sheets. Two Dog, the Indian in *Little Britches,* slept on the ground.

Joe Ed didn't look like he had any diseases.

There were comic books everywhere. Dal sat at the foot of Joe Ed's bed and picked up one called *Buried Alive!* The cover showed a green hand sticking out of the ground. The hand belonged to a dead lady; it had long, sharp fingernails and a diamond ring. People's fingernails kept growing even after they were dead—he had read that somewhere. He turned the pages, mesmerized. When he got to the end, he closed his eyes and took a deep breath. He didn't even want to sleep in the same room as the crude picture of the green hand. Why did horror comics frighten *him* so much and not other kids? Wilbur just sat there, mouthing the words, every once in a while turning the page.

The room was stuffy. Dal was starting to get a headache.

"We could climb out the window," he said to get Wilbur's attention.

"You can if you want to. I'd get the belt."

"Your dad really takes you to the barn and hits you?"

"Bare butt, too," Wilbur said, almost proudly. "Why, don't your mommy and daddy punish you?"

"My mom does sometimes," Dal allowed. "She doesn't hit me with a belt, though."

"You're lucky," Wilbur said, looking at him for one second. Then he put his face back in his comic. "It hurts, too."

Dal had never thought much about it before. When he was little, his mom spanked him sometimes; then they made up with hugs and tears. Dal wondered what he would do if Mr. Sabatini ever tried hitting him. Once, about a month before, Dal had slightly twisted Kate's arm to get her to drop his paint box, which she had been using without his permission. All he did was touch her, but she started screaming bloody murder. The paints were practically ruined: they had all run together in a wash of brown. Dal was in the bathroom, trying to clean them, when Mr. Sabatini called up from the bottom of the stairs that he wanted to see him.

Mr. Sabatini was sitting in his La-Z-Boy lounger, which he had brought with him from their old house. He held the *Detroit News* open on his lap. "Sit down," he said, motioning toward the pink wing chair where Dal's mom usually sat.

Dal tried to explain what had happened, but Mr. Sabatini wouldn't let him finish. He made a speech about how boys were not allowed to hit their little sisters.

"I *didn't* hit her!" Dal said. I should have, though, the spoiled brat, he added in his mind.

"Case closed," Mr. Sabatini said, picking up his newspaper.

When his mother got home, Dal followed her around the kitchen, telling her what had happened. He was pretty sure she would be on his side. But to his surprise she said, "Little sisters want to do everything their older brothers do. You have to be patient." At least she agreed that Kate's temper was something they needed to work on.

After supper, at which nobody said much, Mr. Sabatini casually asked Dal if he wanted to play catch before it got too dark to see the ball. "I guess," Dal said. Unfortunately Kate wanted to play, too. She was so little she missed the ball even when you rolled it. Dal and her dad had to wait patiently while she chased the ball down the street and crawled under parked cars to look for it. Neither of them could think of anything to say.

Knowing that Mr. Dunn hit his own son made Dal feel very sympathetic toward Wilbur, who wasn't that bad, really, once you got to know him.

"You know a girl named Patty Pucket?" he said.

Wilbur still didn't look up from his comic. "I know all the kids from Hazelton," he said. "I hate their guts. They're all stuck up."

Dal could just see Patty coming down the driveway, saying, "Hi, Dal," as if she had known him all her life. Stuck up?

"You know her daddy?" Wilbur said.

"I met him. Len."

Wilbur looked over at Dal and held an invisible bottle to his lips. "He's a drunk," he said gleefully. "One time he got so drunk he tried to burn their house down. That's a fact. He owes my daddy over a hundred dollars. I guess we'll never see that again."

Dal decided not to tell him about the uranium mine.

"You'll see her tomorrow probably."

"Patty? I will? Where?"

"Tomorrow's Tuesday," Wilbur said, turning the page. "Tuesday and Thursday anyone who wants can go swimming at the municipal pool in Twin Falls. The school bus stops in front of our house."

Before Dal could think of any more questions to ask, the hour was up. Mrs. Dunn called upstairs that it was time for lunch. Dal and Wilbur raced each other to the kitchen. Grilled cheese sandwiches!

CHAPTER **15**

THE POOL
IN TWIN FALLS

A school bus did stop the next morning and pick them up. Wilbur held the little ones back until they had looked both ways; then they all raced across the highway. As soon as Missy had climbed the high steps, she ran to the back to join her friends. The driver checked to see that they were all aboard; then she pulled the lever that closed the folding door. She was a short woman, so short she had a cushion under her and had to sit up straight to see out the windshield. She was an Indian. You could tell by her high cheekbones and her black hair. Her name, according to the red stitching on her blouse, was Ruth.

Wilbur said that Dal was staying at their place, but all she said was: "Well, go sit down. This bus isn't moving till y'all take a seat."

The bus was nearly empty. There were maybe eight kids in all. Among them, halfway back, was Patty Pucket. She sat up, her hand on the seat in front of her. "Dal!" she said. "What are you doing here? Sit with us."

He wanted to, but Wilbur and his brother had climbed into the seat just behind the front door.

Dal stood in the aisle, torn.

Patty said something to the girl next to her, who looked at Dal expressionless as she chewed her gum. Then something happened that shocked Dal. Patty stood up and called out, "Hey, Slobber. Why aren't you home milking your cows?" She and her seatmate slid down in their seat so that only their eyes were visible.

Poor Wilbur: when he got excited, a little spit *did* come out of the side of his mouth and run down his chin. He couldn't help it. But what did that say about Dal? Sometimes when he woke up, there was slobber on *his* pillow.

The girl next to Patty put her hand on the seat in front of her. "Hey, Slobber," she called out, "does your little brother slobber, too? What's his name—Drool?"

She and Patty leaned against each other, laughing, while Joe Ed slowly turned around and looked first at Patty and then at Dal. But Wilbur elbowed him, and he turned back around.

Dal was still standing in the middle of the bus, holding on to two seats across from each other, when Ruth said in a calm voice, "You're going to have to take a seat, honey, or I'm going to have to stop this bus. Those are state regulations." She was watching him in the rearview mirror.

Dal held up his hand to Patty and went to join Wilbur and Joe Ed. Wilbur made his brother get up so that Dal could sit next to him. Joe Ed didn't want to, but they couldn't all sit in the same seat. Joe Ed climbed into the seat behind and leaned forward over the seat back so he could hear, too.

"I told you I hated her."

"Well, why don't you call them something back?"

"Like what? 'Ugly'?"

Just then a spit wad sailed over their heads and landed smack on the windshield. Wilbur whirled around, screaming, "Ugly, ugly, ugly!" The girls had disappeared, but you could hear their laughter. Wilbur's face was bright red. He was making whimpering sounds like he was going to have a fit.

Oh, brother, thought Dal. He could feel his heart beating. Turning around, he said as calmly as he could, "Cut it out." He sounded like a teacher. Dal felt sick at heart. Until this minute he had liked Patty a whole lot better than Wilbur. Now he practically hated her.

"That was a Slobber wad," said Patty's seatmate.

Everyone laughed, even Ruth, though she said, "Kids, if I see another spit wad, this bus will turn around and head back to Hazelton."

The rest of the way to Twin Falls, calm reigned. Dal settled back and stared out the window.

Even from the parking lot, the Twin Falls Municipal Pool smelled like a pool. As soon as their bus had pulled alongside the four or five others already parked in the shade and the door folded open, all the kids piled out and ran screaming and hollering across the manicured lawn to the front entrance. You entered a brick building, paid your quarter, got the back of your hand stamped, and then went through the door marked "Boys." There were other boys in there, changing; Dal pretended not to look. A sign said you had to take a shower, but the water was c o l d. Most kids just put their hands and feet in and wet their shoulders. The pool was packed. Kids were screaming, the diving board *boing*ed and *boing*ed, water kept splashing. Dal walked along the cement edge, hypnotized by the pale blue water. He could feel the sun shining on his bare shoulders.

He loitered nonchalantly by the door marked "Girls," but you couldn't see in.

Then out of nowhere Patty appeared beside him. Her yellow bathing suit was already wet, and there were drops of chlorinated water on her freckled cheeks. A few strands of her hair had come loose, and she tucked them back under her bathing cap.

Dal wanted to stay mad at her, but how could he? Her pale blue eyes were looking at him. Standing next to her, he felt like he was on television.

She looked at the backs of her arms, which were covered with goose bumps, then hugged herself. "Aren't you g-going in?" she chattered.

"Are you?"

"I just got out, but I'll go back in if you do."

Without waiting, she took small, mincing steps to the pool's edge, raised her hands over her head, and, bending her knees, dived in. Dal watched her swim across the pool, lifting her head with each stroke. He waited until she had made it to the other side, then dived in after her. For the first few seconds the water was *f-freezing*. Underwater, where it seemed to hum, there was a crowd of pale legs.

He grabbed a pair in his tentacles and hoped they were the right ones. When he came up for air, she was screaming. She used both hands to splash him. He splashed her back. Keeping a storm between them, they gradually worked their way into the deep end, where it was harder to splash and stay afloat.

Patty treaded water. Her thin hand kept darting to the edge of the pool. She had a smear of snot on her upper lip, trailing from her left nostril. Snot nose! thought Dal.

Wilbur waved to him from the shallow end, where he looked like he was sitting in a giant bathtub. Dal waved back.

"Why are you guys so mean to him?"

"Because he's weird. Look at him."

"He can't swim probably. That doesn't make him weird."

"He is, though. Wait and see."

Dal gave her a look, but she didn't seem to notice. A minute ago she was cute, but now, like Wilbur said, she *was* kind of ugly, a skinny girl with pale, freckled skin. At least her bathing cap and yellow bathing suit were ugly.

"He may be a little strange," Dal said, "but he's not weird."

"How come you're staying with him?"

"They invited me to. I'm going to go horseback riding."

"His momma's even more stranger than he is. That whole family's strange."

"Maybe you'd be strange, too, if you grew up in that family."

"I would. If Mr. Dunn was my daddy, I'd be mental. He tried to run my daddy over once."

"You're kidding."

She shook her head. "He goes berserk."

Dal watched Joe Ed, who was waiting patiently in line for the diving board. When it was his turn, he ran to the end, held his nose, and jumped in the water.

"Joe Ed doesn't seem that bad. He's a nice kid."

"Joe Ed is the only one of the bunch who's not crazy," Patty said.

With that she swam away with her neat little stroke, swinging her head from side to side. Dal watched as she crossed the pool. When she reached the other side, she boosted herself up, belly first, and climbed out. Carefully she peeled her bathing cap up over her ears and dried the ends of her hair with a towel. The reddish blond strands sparkled in the sunshine.

How could I have thought she was ugly? Dal thought, treading water.

Now she spread her towel on the ground, dropped to her knees, and stretched out on her stomach, propping her face on her fists. She squinted at the water, trying to find him. When she did, she waved. That was enough for Dal. He took a deep breath, pushed off from the side, and swam toward her with all his might.

Nobody said much on the way home. It was too hot. The first stop was the Dunns' place. Before following his brother and sister out the door, Wilbur called out, "Hey, Patty. There's a fungus among us. Kill it before it multiplies." Everybody was saying that that summer. Whimpering with laughter, Wilbur stomped down the steps with Dal behind him.

Supper that night was a macaroni and cheese and string bean casserole, bread and butter piled on a pink plastic plate, and Neapolitan ice cream for dessert. Mr. Dunn joined them at the kitchen table, nodding solemnly at Dal. He didn't say a word to anyone, just sat with one hand on his knife and the other hand on his fork, while Mrs. Dunn burned her thumb trying to get the casserole out of the oven. She served her husband first. As soon as his plate was set before him, he lowered his face over the steaming macaroni and began shoveling it into his mouth.

Dal noticed that although his hands were red from the sun, the creases filled with grime, they were surprisingly neat-looking, wiry. He would have expected a farmer's hands to look like old gloves. His hat must have sat on his head in the same place all day because a band of gray skin went around his forehead. Below that mark, his face and neck were fiery red; his eyes baby blue.

For several minutes, while everyone else was being served, nobody said a word, except when Mrs. Dunn said in an angry whisper to Missy, "Guests first." She held a plate up near her bosom, then handed it to Dal.

Wilbur, whose mouth was full of bread and butter, broke the silence by saying, "Pafth a milk."

His father put down his knife and fork with a sigh and lifted up the pitcher of milk. For a second he looked like he was going to hurl it at his son, but he merely gave it to Joe Ed, who took it in both hands and passed it on. As the pitcher made its way toward him, Dal eyed the watery contents suspiciously, wondering if he dare ask for tap water instead.

After Mrs. Dunn had mushed up a spoonful of casserole in a little blue bowl, she finally sat down and began feeding the baby. Even the baby seemed subdued tonight, gumming her supper with a philosophical look. After a while Mrs. Dunn looked over her shoulder and said, "Missy lost her bathing suit—that pretty one with the polka dots? It cost nearly five dollars."

Mr. Dunn scowled. "Pass the bread," he said.

The bread plate was in front of Dal. He got to pass it. When it reached the man of the house, he nodded once and said, "I thank you."

"I didn't *lose* it," Missy said, sighing a huge sigh. "Someone *stoled* it."

"How could somebody stole your bathing suit, dummy?" Wilbur said. "You was wearing it."

"Not all the time I wasn't, dummy. I had to put my stupid dress on."

Mr. Dunn reached his knife across the table and took a swipe of butter. Having buttered his bread, he folded it in half and slowly began to chew it. The kitchen clock ticked, one tick for every second, sixty ticks per minute. When the second hand reached twelve, as if on cue, the baby stood up in her chair and banged her tray with her spoon. Mrs. Dunn snatched it away, holding it over her shoulder warningly. The baby scrunched up her face like she was going to howl. Mr. Dunn leaned back in his chair and used one of his fingernails to pick his teeth. "Looks to me like somebody had better find it," he said in a gentle, almost laughing voice.

"I told her we'd find it," said Wilbur. He glared at his mother. "Tattletale. I told you, all you got to do is go up to the desk and ask have they found it. It'll be in the lost and found."

"Not if it's stoled," said Missy.

"Somebody m-might have took it, thinking it was theirs," said Joe Ed, fork in hand. "That wouldn't be stealing."

His mother looked at her husband. "You all, some of us are tired of hearing about bathing suits. You should have checked, Wilbur. She's your little sister."

"She had her towel rolled up," said Wilbur, his voice rising. "How was I supposed to know it wasn't inside?"

"That's enough," said Mrs. Dunn. "Don't you see your daddy's tired?"

"Yes'um."

Dal watched in fascination as Mr. Dunn drank a whole glass of milk in a single draft, his Adam's apple bobbing up and down. He set the empty glass down and wiped his mouth with his hand.

"Them beans are gone dry," he observed, as if beans had been the topic of conversation and not polka-dotted bathing suits. At first Dal thought he was criticizing his wife's cooking, but sixty ticks later Mr. Dunn added, "Goin' to have to divert some irrigation water up there."

The clock filled the silence that followed this remark.

"Well, I need some grocery money," Mrs. Dunn said.

The kids were quiet now, except for Missy, fussing at Joe Ed. Their hands were under the table, both pairs of eyes on their dad. Wilbur reached around his brother and hit Missy on the back of her head. She winced and held her head with both hands as if it were "broke"—that was the word she mouthed. She shook her face at Wilbur, but neither of them said a word.

Mr. Dunn chuckled, and Dal was so relieved he almost did, too. "Horse needs a shoe," Mr. Dunn said. "Gosh darn, you should have seen him." He chuckled some more.

"We ain't got no food in the house, hardly. And I have a guest to feed."

"Faubus can shoe that horse first thing tomorrow morning. It come half off in the mud."

"Can we ride him?" said Wilbur, bouncing around in his chair. "Please? Please? Dal's never been on a horse."

"Once," Dal said.

"If I had fifteen or twenty dollars, I could drive into town in the morning. Wilbur will mind the baby."

"I'm not minding no baby. Me and Dal want to ride the horse, don't we, Dal?" He added in a stage whisper, "Say yes."

"So do I," said Missy, lining her knife and spoon on either side of her plate.

"S-so do I," said Joe Ed.

"Well, take you ten dollars, but it's to last till Saturday."

"For fifteen I could get something nice for our guest. I could get him some hot dogs."

"I'm fine," said Dal, holding up his hands.

The conversation went on like that, like a couple of old peepers playing leapfrog with each other on a warm summer night.

When supper was over, Dal offered to help with the dishes, but Mrs. Dunn reminded him that he was the guest.

Dal thought he was never going to fall asleep that night. It was too quiet in the country. You could hear everything: water gurgling in a pipe, somebody coughing down the hall. The rooster crowed once, long before dawn, and a cow said, "Mooo." Wilbur in the next bed whimpered in his sleep. (Was it really true, Dal wondered, that if you put a person's hand in warm water while he was sleeping, he would pee in his bed?) Suddenly, from down the hall, Missy went, "No, no, no, no, no!" and then she started crying to herself. Dal expected somebody to get up and rub her back and sing her a bedtime song—that was what his mom did when he had a nightmare. But the rest of the house stayed quiet. After a while she stopped.

CHAPTER 16

ON HORSEBACK

Next day, when their chores were done, Wilbur took Dal to see the Snake River Canyon, which ran right through their property. There was nothing to warn a person that danger lay ahead: no sign or fence. One minute they had been walking through a bean field; the next, the ground opened up under their feet. "Gosh!" Dal said, peering carefully over the edge. Where the beans had been, there was nothing, neither ground nor sky, just a great crack that split the earth in two. On the other side, maybe a hundred yards across, the beans resumed, row upon row.

"That your field, too?"

"It's my daddy's."

"How does he get across?"

Wilbur looped a strap of his overalls over his meaty shoulder. "It's a long ride to the bridge," he said.

Dal dropped down in the warm dirt. He wriggled forward on his stomach until his chin hung over the cliff. The warm air was dizzying. Far below lay the Snake River. You could see how it got its name, winding through the earth's crust. From this height it looked harmless enough, a mere trickle. But Dal had heard time and again how it was the source for the whole Magic Valley. Without its waters the Dunns' farm—all the farms up and down its length—would turn back into cactus and sagebrush.

"If you fell down that, your head would *splat* like a big old watermelon," Wilbur observed philosophically.

Back at the house Mrs. Dunn and the younger kids were waiting in their '49 Ford station wagon to go shopping. "Come on, Wilbur!" Missy whined, leaning out the window as far as she could. "We're tired of waiting on y'all."

They drove to Hazelton, where Mrs. Dunn made them wait in the hot car while she ran into the drugstore for "just a second," which turned out to be more like half an hour. Dal was sitting in the front seat, his head and arm out the window. He kept hoping that Patty Pucket would come out of one of the stores. Instead Mr. Sabatini did. "Wait for me," Dal said, opening his door and getting out.

"Where you going?" asked Wilbur from the backseat. He held the baby in a heap on his lap.

"I'll be back in a second."

Dal leaped up onto the sidewalk and ran after his stepfather. "Hey!" he called out.

Mr. Sabatini spun around. He was eating a chocolate ice cream cone. "Dal," he said, using his bandanna to wipe his mouth. They stood there for a couple of seconds, as if neither of them could think of what to say. Both were wearing their cowboy hats. Finally Mr. Sabatini held out his cone. "Want a lick?" he asked.

Dal put his head down and took a bite, not a lick, because he knew he could. He had so much cold ice cream in his mouth that he could hardly keep from laughing.

Mr. Sabatini's brown eyes twinkled, but all he said was: "How are things going?"

"Okay, I guesh," said Dal, swallowing chocolate ice cream and licking his lips. "We're going shopping."

"Have you been horseback riding yet?"

"Today I'm supposed to."

"I'll come and get you Friday, right after work."

"I know."

Dal called out, "See you," and ran back to the station wagon, which was *ha-ha-hot* as blazes.

In the afternoon Faubus came up from the fields, riding a horse. Its name was Colonel Moore. The hired hand swung his left foot over the horse's back and slid off, leaving heel prints in the mud. He smoked the stump of a cigarette; it was a wonder it didn't burn the side of his mouth, where it was tucked. Gripping the horse by his bridle, he walked him over to where the boys were standing.

"You going to ride him?" he said to Dal. The horse, a wild look in his eyes, tried wrenching his head away from Faubus's firm hand and took a lively step backward.

Dal's heart was beating inside his white T-shirt like a trapped bird. "I'd like to," he lied.

"Well, climb up then. Other side, other side."

"I've only ridden once before." Dal managed to lift his foot into the stirrup. He put one hand on the saddle and the other in the horse's bristly hair and tried to pull himself up. The saddle had the sweet smell of old, much-used leather. Faubus and Wilbur gave him a boost from behind. *Oomph:* he was up, sitting high above the barnyard and its inhabitants like young George Washington. He was scared and thrilled.

Faubus adjusted the length of the stirrups. "That about suit you?" he asked. "I'll walk you around till you get the hang of it."

"Can I ride next? Can I ride next?" Wilbur chanted.

"Your daddy said *he* was to ride. He didn't say nothin' about you."

With Faubus holding on to his bridle, the animal seemed indifferent to the boy on his back. He put out one long leg after another and followed Faubus around the yard. Dal wasn't quite sure what he was supposed to hold on to. He kept one hand on the reins and one on the pommel, but it seemed like there should be a steering wheel or a handle that you could get a real grip on. Each step the Colonel took jostled Dal slightly off-balance. Instinctively he tightened his knees. The horse responded by stepping in a livelier fashion.

"You want to take him for a canter, you can," Faubus said, opening a wide gate that the boys had swung on earlier. Ahead lay pasture, fields, the open country.

"Here," said Faubus, straightening the reins in Dal's hands, showing him how to hold them. He still had that mite of a cigarette tucked in the corner of his mouth. "Pull which way you want him to go," he said through his closed lips. "Pull back to stop him. He's a smart animal. He knows what to do."

The smart animal stood there, swishing his tail and stretching his neck. He made his skin twitch to shoo away flies.

"Come on, boy," Dal said softly, jiggling the reins. With a long, loping gait, the horse walked forward, a little faster than Dal wished.

"That's it," said Faubus's voice, already yards away.

Dal had never felt more alive in his life. Added to his regular body was the loudly breathing body of the animal between his legs. He was a centaur. And he was so high up—why does height make a person feel powerful? He tried to steer Colonel Moore around a cow pie, but when he tugged on the reins, the horse tugged back and swung his great head around to see who was sitting on him. "It's me," said Dal, excitement bubbling up in him. He patted the Colonel on his long neck. "You're a good horse. I like you."

The Colonel started trot, trot, trotting. Each trot meant Dal was lifted from his seat and brought back down with a spank. Maybe faster would be better. "Giddyup," Dal said softly in the horse's ear, giving the Colonel's flanks an experimental kick with both heels. The Colonel didn't wait for more instructions but broke into a canter. Where they were supposed to be headed, Dal had no idea. His only thought was to stay on. He leaned as far forward as he could, bent his legs back, and said a prayer: "Help!" The horse turned a windless day into a cyclone. The air growled in Dal's ears. He felt like he was on the Flying Red Horse—only the horse was gray, not red.

If in some part of his mind Dal could think, This is fun—*darump, darump, darump, darump*—first and foremost he knew that he was out of control. He had no idea how to steer this galloping beast, let alone stop him. Pulling back on the reins only seemed to make him go faster. He kept thinking that around here somewhere was the Snake River Canyon. No real horse could fly across that mighty chasm. When the time came, Dal would do his best to stay on, as the horse, dancing on empty air, fell to the river miles below: *splat.*

But when Colonel Moore reached the poplars that bordered the pasture, he turned and ran alongside them, and when he came to the wooden fence, he turned again and headed back to the farm buildings.

"Stop!" Dal said to the wind. "That's enough already. Quit it. Trot, trot." He felt like swearing. "Darn you," he said, sitting up and pulling on the reins with all his might. "Wooah." *Darump, darump, da-rump, daaah-rump.* In the final seconds the horse slowed to a walk and stepped neatly through the wide open gate and back into the yard. Dal, still alive, clung to the Colonel's back.

He wished like anything that Mr. Sabatini was there to see him. Faubus was examining the sole of his boot. Wilbur had mounted the fence and was facing the other way, shaking invisible reins up and down. Missy came down the back steps with a purple Popsicle, from which she carefully removed the paper and dropped it on the ground.

The horse stopped, took a step backward, and lowered his head. Dal gladly lifted his right gym shoe high over the Colonel's neck, flipped onto his belly, and slid all the way to the hard, stinging ground.

"You stayed on," Faubus said, still sucking on the cigarette in the corner of his mouth. He took the reins from Dal. There might have been a smile on his frog face—it was hard to tell. "Truth is, I didn't expect you would."

Dal wondered what the hired hand *had* expected.

Wilbur climbed down from the fence. He said he didn't want to ride after all.

"Good thing, too," said Faubus, puffing on his cigarette. "Break the poor animal's back."

Friday evening, getting close to suppertime, the green pickup drove into the Dunns' yard. Dal was ready and waiting. Wilbur, sitting on a tricycle that was much too small for him, dragged himself forward with his long legs. From deep inside his voice box he made engine sounds.

Mr. Sabatini pushed his hat back on his head and smiled his trademark smile (showing all his teeth). Dal went up to him, holding his suitcase in both hands. "Throw it in the back," his stepfather said, and went over and shook hands with Wilbur and his brother and sister—they were there, too. Mrs. Dunn came down the back steps, carrying the baby.

"I sure appreciate everything you've done," Mr. Sabatini said, taking off his hat. Dal noticed that the longer they stayed in Idaho, the more Mr. Sabatini sounded like an Idahoan.

Dal couldn't be sure, but out of the corner of his eye he seemed to see Mr. Sabatini slip an envelope into Mrs. Dunn's hand. But if so, where did it go? When Dal stepped up to his hostess to say, "Thanks for everything. I had a nice time," there was no envelope in sight.

"He wasn't no bother. He can come again if he wants to," she said.

Dal was eager to get going. He got in the truck and slammed the door. Through the open window he could still talk to Wilbur, who had climbed up on the running board. Mr. Sabatini was saying something to Mrs. Dunn. Missy was holding the baby, a sagging armful with an alarmingly red face. The evening was still; the cooling air smelled of cut grass. Dal gave the horn a polite beep.

Mr. Sabatini called out good-bye for the hundredth time and got in the truck. Wilbur and Joe Ed ran alongside the length of the driveway. They stood at the edge of the highway and waved. The truck turned right, toward Hazelton. "Hungry?" Mr. Sabatini said.

"Starved!" said Dal.

URANIUM FEVER

All of a sudden Dal and Mr. Sabatini had something to talk about: uranium. They became authorities on the subject, even stopping off at the Hazelton library to see what the big dictionary had to say. "Uranium," Dal read over Mr. Sabatini's shoulder. "Symbol U, a heavy silvery-white metallic, radioactive element, occurring in several minerals, such as pitchblende and carnotite, from which it is extracted and processed."

Mostly they "spent" the vast sums of money they would make from their mine. Mr. Sabatini was going to open a garden center, smack-dab in the middle of Detroit, with factories on all sides.

"I'd have everything the urban gardener could need," he told Dal as they drove down a dirt road with the windows wide open. "Think how beautiful our downtown neighborhoods could be with flowers and vegetables in everybody's backyard. Maybe someday you'll want to come in on the business," he added shyly. "Sabatini and Son. After you're through with school, of course."

"Maybe."

Dal was going to spend his share on a horse and call it Sagebrush Patty. He hadn't completely forgotten how scared he had been on horseback, but mostly he remembered the excitement.

"Where you going to keep her?"

"In the garage?"

"Uh, I don't think horses are allowed in town. Maybe we could board her in the country. I could drive you and Kate out on week-ends to ride her."

Dal looked at the fields flying past. "If I had enough money, I could buy her a pony and call it Peek-a-boo."

Then something happened that put a wrinkle in their plans. Len Pucket disappeared. Conchita, the chambermaid, went into Number 7 to clean up as usual and found the place empty, stripped bare. Gone was the framed picture of the mountain lion. Even the sardine can ashtray was missing. He had taken off late one night or early one morning without telling a soul where he was going—not his partners in the mine, not even old Mrs. Pucket.

"He may be in Washington in secret negotiations," said Jerry Foster.

"Or at the mine site, excavating," said Mr. Sabatini.

"Or in Mexico," said Margaret.

"Or in Timbuktu," said Patty.

They were over the Fosters', eating Margaret's famous spaghetti and meatballs. That was the summer Dal learned to like spaghetti.

"Harry's right," Jerry said. "This doesn't mean a blamed thing. Len Pucket has always been a loner. I have a certificate that says I'm part owner of a uranium mine. It's signed and sealed. I called the bank in Idaho Falls: it really exists. That's good enough for me."

"Does it say you'll ever see a penny of that hundred dollars you gave him?"

"It was an investment, Margaret. I have my shares. Legally I'm part owner."

"And how do you know those rocks came from his old silver mine? How do you know he didn't just buy them from a rock shop? Jerry Foster, have you ever before in your life given any money to Len Pucket?"

"Oh, a few dollars, here and there. Mostly small loans in times of need. You know that."

"And have you ever, ever, ever gotten one penny of that money back?"

"He gave us that oil painting of a doe and her fawn to settle a gambling debt."

Dal felt embarrassed for Patty. Everybody was saying mean things about her father, as if she wasn't there. But she didn't seem to mind. In fact, she kept making bug eyes at Dal, as if she was trying to tell him something.

After supper Margaret said, "Why don't you two go out and play?" and put them out with Sheppy.

It was a night of crickets. They lingered on the back porch to pet the dog. When their hands touched accidentally, Dal felt squishy inside. They could hear snatches of conversation through the kitchen door.

Mr. Sabatini said, "If we could drive down there and see the mine with our own two eyes, I'd feel a lot better."

"That's a good idea," said Jerry Foster.

"It's a loony idea," said his wife.

Patty stood up and slapped her hands clean of dog fur. "Come on," she said in a low voice. "I want to show you something."

"Who told Margaret?" Dal asked, following her through the bushes. He felt like running and skipping. "I thought it was supposed to be top secret."

"*He* did. Jerry Foster has never been able to keep a secret in his life. If he ever did anything bad, like murder somebody, the first thing he'd do is come in, paw the floor, and tell her down to every last detail." Doing funny things with her chin, she added in a deep voice, "*I shot that no-good son of a gun, Margaret. A fellow as low as him don't deserve to live.*"

"Gosh," said Dal. "But I thought she'd be mad if she knew."

"She is. She wants to bean him."

"Where do you think your dad is?"

"He's around."

She didn't seem to be bothered one bit, dancing sideways down the rutted driveway, under poplars rolled up like umbrellas against the stars. The barn was a silent ship in the night. Behind it was a great burrow that sloped underground. Dal had seen others like it and knew what it was: a spud cellar. Farmers stored their famous Idaho potatoes in the cool dirt. Patty unlatched the heavy metal door, let it swing open like an old gate, and disappeared inside. Dal hesitated: it was pitch black in there. Patty came back out and said in a loud whisper, "You coming or not?"

He stepped carefully, holding his hand in front of his face. The air inside smelled moldy. Two feeble lightbulbs came on overhead. Patty climbed down from the chair she had used to reach the switch. In the dim light the spud cellar looked calm and purposeful. There was no green hand reaching up from its grave, just shovels and pitchforks parked against the walls, wooden boxes, and burlap sacks.

At the far end was a sawhorse, and beyond it a big hole, darker than the cellar. "Careful," Patty said, putting her hands out. Dal walked right into one of them, accidentally on purpose, and tried to see into the hole. "That's where the bomb shelter is going to be," Patty said. "It's going to have beds and everything."

Dal's face was about three inches from hers. He could just nonchalantly kiss her, if he wanted to. "Why would anyone want to bomb Idaho?" he asked right in her ear.

"I don't know," said Patty, ducking away. "They might, though. To destroy Len's uranium mine, if they found out about it."

She climbed back on the chair to turn the light off. They went and stood just inside the doorway to the spud cellar. "Look," she said, pointing at the night sky. "We've been bombed."

Dal could feel her next to him, a living, breathing human being.

"Yeah," he managed to say, "our guys bombed their guys, and their guys bombed our guys. A cloud of deadly radioactive smoke has spread over the whole world."

Patty made explosive sounds with her mouth, like distant bombs falling. She started to walk through the door, but Dal clapped his hand on her shoulder. "Don't go out there! Don't you know the air is radioactive? If you breathe it for more than about ten seconds, you're a goner. Luckily we're protected by our invisible shield." He knocked with his knuckle on the thin air of the doorway.

Patty looked at him with shining eyes. He still had his hand on her shoulder. She waited for a couple of seconds, and then she said, "Everybody else is dead, even my mama. C. J. McAdoo has been burnt to a crisp."

"*My* stepdad got away," said Dal, out of breath. "He was in his pickup and rolled up his windows. Luckily they were made of mica. Don't!" he cried, but Patty shrugged away from his hand and walked out under the stars. She positioned herself just so and did a cartwheel across the yard. How did she do it? Dal wondered, following her out. If he put his hands out and tried, his feet would stick to the ground. The most he would be able to do would be kick one foot up in the air (he knew; he had tried). She cartwheeled back.

He walked right up to her, leaned forward toward her cheek, but she spun away. "We've been bombed!" she crowed. "We've been bombed!"

Dal had to swallow before he could speak again. "Maybe we could find some old tin cans and make oxygen masks."

"We don't need to," Patty said, taking deep breaths right in his face to show she wasn't afraid of breathing radioactive air. "We waited six months in the bomb shelter. By now it's safe to come out. See?"

"What about Sheppy and the cats?"

"We rescued them. They were in the bomb shelter with us. Don't you remember?"

"Oh, yeah," said Dal.

"There are only two people left alive. You"—she pushed him in the chest—"and me. Know what that means?"

He was pretty sure he did. It meant he could kiss her, maybe hold her hand, and she would let him. But when he stepped toward her again, she slipped away, laughing. In the dark her voice said, "You have to catch me first."

Oh, brother, he thought.

Just then Mr. Sabatini's whistle sounded. The crickets grew quiet. "Patty!" Dal shouted. "I have to go in." But Patty was nowhere to be seen. Dal walked around the barn, checked under the trucks, behind the farm machines. He finally found her in the kitchen with the others. She wouldn't look at him, even though she kept using her hand to wipe the smile off her face.

He was in time to hear Mr. Sabatini say, "I'm telling you, the only way any of us are ever going to know for sure is to rent a Geiger counter, drive down there, and switch it on."

CHAPTER 18

HUNTING FOR TREASURE

Margaret Foster said that Jerry wasn't going to Rattler's Gulch to look for a uranium mine that probably didn't exist anyway. "Aw, Margaret," he said. And she strongly advised Mr. Sabatini and Dal not to go on a wild-goose chase, either. Mr. Sabatini laughed. "The worst thing that can happen to us, Margaret, is that we'll get lost in the desert."

"Worse things than that can happen," she said darkly.

The trip to the mine was on! Dal asked if Wilbur could come, too. "Please? He never gets to go anywhere."

Mr. Sabatini seemed a little surprised. "That boy looks kind of soft to me. Does he know we'll be roughing it?"

"You gotta give people the benefit of the doubt," Dal said, trying not to smile.

Jerry procured a Geiger counter from somewhere as well as a government survey map, which he rolled out on his desk. Dal and Mr. Sabatini looked over his shoulder. The mine area was off the main road, down near the Utah border. The nearest town was Beulah, only it had a line drawn through it. "Ghost town," Jerry said. "Nobody's lived there for thirty years or more. Not enough water. There are a few small ranches, mostly Mormons. The rest is desert."

Friday after work they stopped at the Dunns' place, and Wilbur appeared on the back steps, lugging an oversize suitcase.

"Jeez, we're only going for one night," said Dal through the open window.

"Shh," his stepfather said, putting a hand on Dal's knee. Mr. Sabatini got out and told Wilbur to "heave her in back." Then he talked to Wilbur's mom for about ten years. They would be extra careful, he assured her. There were no bobcats where they were going. The boys certainly wouldn't be allowed to go down any abandoned mine shafts without adult supervision.

Dal and Wilbur waited in the back of the truck in a cocoon of bedrolls.

"Come on, Ma," shouted Wilbur. "We want to get going."

"Behave yourself, Wilbur Dunn, if you ever want to go on a camping trip again."

Wilbur shook his fist at his mother but said he would.

Once they were under way, Dal didn't feel like stopping at the Fosters', but that was the plan. Mr. Foster was going to lend them his jerry can full of spring water so they wouldn't die of thirst. And Mrs. Foster had fixed them their last supper so at least they could die with their stomachs full.

An orange cat waited under a tractor. When Sheppy came limping out to bark once or twice, his tail wagging, the cat withdrew into the dark until only its eyes were visible. Dal jumped down from the pickup. Maybe Patty would be there. He knocked on the back door and went in. The kitchen was bright with sunflowers peering in the windows. Mrs. Foster put an apron on Dal that was way too big for him. She said, "Think you can chop these green onions without cutting off your fingers?"

"I'll try."

"Where's Wilbur Dunn? I thought he was coming."

He was out on the porch. "What are you doing out there?" Dal asked him through the screen. "We have to chop onions."

"Nuts to that," said Wilbur. "We're guests."

But he came inside anyway.

"Here," Dal said, "you have to wear this." He hung the apron on Wilbur's neck. It was too small for him.

"Wilbur Dunn, how you've grown," said Mrs. Foster by way of greeting. "Your folks doing okay?"

"Yes, ma'am."

"Where's Patty?" Dal asked, as nonchalantly as he could.

"Uh, I don't think we'll be seeing her around here tonight. She's mad."

"At me?"

"Mad at everybody. She's mad at you because your daddy is taking you out to that god-forsaken snake hole. She's mad at me, I reckon, because I'm the one that told her she can't go. I'd tell *you* you couldn't go, but you have to listen to your stepdaddy, even if he is a darn fool."

Dal volunteered to go over to Patty's house and talk to her, but Mrs. Foster said, "She'll come over if and when she feels like it."

At supper, in the dining room, Mr. Sabatini said how delicious everything tasted. The boys said so, too. Chicken and dumplings. Mr. Sabatini asked Mrs. Foster how her people happened to end up in Idaho, and she wiped her mouth on her napkin and got up from the table. While she was gone, Wilbur stared at his plate and Mr. Foster just smiled. In a minute she was back with an old black doctor's bag.

"This is how my daddy ended up in Idaho." She lifted the bag onto the table with a thump. "He had a horse and buggy and this bag, and he went around doctoring people. If you're pigheaded enough to go looking for that mine, you'd better take this along."

Dal and Wilbur got up to look, as Mrs. Foster released the catch and opened the top half into two wings. Every corner was cleverly fitted with something useful to a doctor: small stoppered vials tucked into a rack of holes, packets of gauze in a cloth envelope that snapped shut, scissors in various shapes and sizes, neatly held in place by rubber bands and embedded in the case.

"This," she said, plunking a jar like an ink bottle down on the table, "is good for snakebites; only if you get bitten by a diamondback, you'd be better off with a shovel—to dig a hole with. By the time you get back to civilization, the venom will have spread throughout your whole body. But don't let me tell you your business. If it's the bite of an ordinary snake, this'll bring the swelling down." She unscrewed the lid and sniffed the contents, then held it up under their noses. It smelled like stuff you put on mosquito bites.

She threw a canvas pouch on the table. It had bandages of different sizes on metal spools. "And this," she said, "is to make a splint with, in case one of you falls down a mine shaft and breaks your leg."

Mr. Sabatini backed the pickup around and started down the driveway. Mr. Foster had his arm around Mrs. Foster. The boys shouted, "Bye!" out the window. They were shouting because *finally* they were on their way. Dal navigated; he was getting good at reading maps. Near Heyburn they crossed the river and headed south, away from the valley and into the desert. The sun had set, but pink remnants streaked the sky almost until they reached their campground in the Sawtooth National Forest. Other campers had already pitched their tents. Their campfires flickered through the trees. Mr. Sabatini stopped at the ranger station to register, then drove to their assigned site. Dal was beginning to get carsick, so as soon as the truck stopped, he opened the door and jumped out. In the same moment somebody jumped off the back of the truck and quickly stepped into the shadows.

"Patty!" said Dal.

By now the others had seen her, too. "A stowaway," Mr. Sabatini said.

Wilbur cried, "You're going to get a licking!" He stuffed his big arms in the bib of his overalls.

"Am not, fatso," Patty said. Her voice carried in the night air.

"Are you mad at me, Mr. Sabatini? I had to come, too. I'm the only one who knows how to get to the mine."

"Your grandmother gave us directions," said Mr. Sabatini.

Patty smiled her cute smile: she sort of wrinkled up her nose and looked like she knew something no one else did.

"Okay," said Mr. Sabatini. "So the directions aren't a hundred percent accurate?"

"I know how to get to the mine," Patty said again. She had ambled over to where they were standing.

The kids looked at Mr. Sabatini. He was shaking his head, a slight smile on his mouth. It sure wasn't fair, Dal thought; if he had tried something like that, he'd be in trouble. Girls got away with murder. Then it occurred to Dal that Mr. Sabatini must like Patty, too. He was saying, "You're going to have to call the Fosters and let them know you're okay."

"Gee, thanks, Mr. Sabatini."

"Aren't you going to give her a licking?" said Wilbur.

"But where's she going to sleep?" Dal asked. "You have a bedroll, Patty?"

"I can sleep in the truck. I ain't cold."

They drove back to the public showers, where there was a pay phone outside. Mr. Sabatini emptied his pockets and held all the nickels and dimes and quarters out in front of him in both hands. Dal contributed fifteen cents. Patty plucked the coins she needed and fed them into the coin slot. She told the honest truth. "Please don't be mad at me," she said. You could hear Margaret Foster's voice on the other end, whooping and hollering.

Wilbur stood behind Dal's shoulder and said gleefully, "She's going to get a licking."

Mr. Sabatini took the phone. "No, no trouble in the world. Glad to have her." He winked at Patty; her teeth were gleaming.

Dal felt like the luckiest boy alive.

"Now don't you worry," said Mr. Sabatini.

He shook his head as he hung up, but he said, "It's okay."

"Yea!" they all shouted, even Wilbur. Patty did a cartwheel right in the road.

It was a star-filled night, the moon a giant toenail in the sky. Dal wondered if anyone else had ever thought that. As they were gathering wood for a fire, he blurted out, "It looks like a toenail."

"What does?" said Wilbur.

"The moon."

"No, it doesn't, Dal. It looks like the moon. Jeez."

When the campfire had burned down to embers, they sat around toasting marshmallows. Wilbur was too impatient to toast his, and each one went up in flames. Mr. Sabatini didn't usually feel like talking about the war, but that night he told them about the time his ship got torpedoed. The sailors had to swim for their lives—underwater because the oil on the surface had caught on fire. He got down on his hands and knees to demonstrate the stroke he'd used—a sort of bunched-up breaststroke—holding his breath for as long as he could and coming up through the fire for quick gulps of air.

It wasn't funny when you thought about it, but the kids rocked with laughter. So did Mr. Sabatini. Then he stood up and kicked dirt over the embers to smother them. "Better hit the sack."

Dal didn't want the story to end, so he quickly asked, "But how'd you get away?"

"Oh." Mr. Sabatini stopped his boot in mid-motion. "We just kept swimming and swimming, until the fire was far behind us. Luckily there was enough of a moon to see by, like tonight. To this day I have no idea what we grabbed hold of, but whatever it was kept us afloat. We held on till dawn's early light, when we were spotted by one of our own ships. You know, you're not beaten till you think you are."

Dal let Patty have his bedroll. "I don't need one," she said, but Mr. Sabatini said, "You will later on. It'll get cold before morning."

Patty and Wilbur announced that they were deathly afraid of snakes, so Patty slept in the cab, and after Mr. Sabatini said he had never heard of a snake climbing up the wheels, Wilbur slept in the back of the truck.

Dal and his stepdad laid the tarp out on the ground. They spread the remaining bedroll over it, opened up. Then they settled down on top and covered themselves with sweatshirts. Dal left his jeans on because he didn't want Patty to see his underpants. He said he wasn't afraid of snakes, but he kept checking to be on the safe side.

They set out early the next morning, Patty and Wilbur in back. Dal had the map open on his lap. They were headed to the southeastern corner of the state. The road led down from the hills back into the valley. There were funny-looking dirt formations—mesas, his stepfather called them. They drove right though the middle of one. It was a hill with the top down, a convertible. All Dal could get on the radio was gospel music from Salt Lake City—they sure were a long way from Eden. They stopped at a gas station that said LAST CHANCE TO FILL UP FOR 40 MILES and CLEAN PUBLIC REST ROOMS, but the bathrooms weren't clean; they stank. Patty came out of the ladies' holding her nose.

The only signs of civilization now were the black tar road they were on and the telephone poles looped together with wires. Everywhere was sagebrush. At first it was easy to follow the map. The road had a number that corresponded to a thin blue line on the map. The sun was on the left, sort of in their eyes. Dal knew that that meant they were going southeast. But then they turned onto a dirt road that wasn't on the map and led straight to the middle of nowhere.

Mr. Sabatini pulled to one side and stopped, and a cloud of dust floated in the open windows. He leaned his head out and said something to Patty. She came around and got in front, too. Wilbur said he was fine where he was. When they started up again, he stretched out on top of Dal's bedroll and closed his eyes.

"Hi," said Patty, smiling at Dal.

They had already said hi to each other, but Dal said hi again anyway.

She sat forward on the seat with her hand on the dashboard. She had freckles up her arms and on her shoulders and everywhere. Dal only had about six freckles on his whole body.

They passed the old carcass of an abandoned car. It was just sitting on its bare rims in the dirt, not going anywhere in a hurry. Dal looked out the back window. It would be fun to play in, pretend drive.

The road kept on and on. "You sure you're going to know when we get there?" Mr. Sabatini said.

Patty nodded.

"I take it you've been here before?"

"When I was little."

"So what's your opinion? You think there's uranium in this mine?"

Patty looked very serious. She blew some hair out of her eyes, then brushed it back impatiently with her hand. "Len does," she said, staring through the windshield.

After a while Mr. Sabatini said, "You see that?"

"What?" said Dal and Patty together.

Wilbur thumped on the cab top. "You see that?" he cried.

Mr. Sabatini stopped the truck and backed up.

"What?" said Dal, trying to see out his stepdad's window. Three ugly birds were feasting on a chunk of bright red meat. When the truck stopped and Wilbur jumped down, the birds flapped their wings and swooped in a circle overhead. They landed and began hopping back to whatever it was they were eating.

"Get back in the truck, Wilbur," Mr. Sabatini cried. "They can be vicious."

"Buzzards," Wilbur announced, climbing back up. He shouted something at them, and they answered with equally rude cries.

Patty didn't want to look, once she had seen what it was. "Was it a deer?"

"Hard to tell," Mr. Sabatini said.

Patty had tears in her eyes. "Please let's go."

In the back they could hear Wilbur going, "Gor! You see that?"

They drove another mile or so in silence. Patty used the collar of her shirt to wipe her eyes. Dal watched her surreptitiously.

She pointed. "See that hill? You have to drive up there."

"You kidding me or what? Up there? There's no road."

"Yes, there is." She smiled a little smile. "You'll see. Just keep going."

Mr. Sabatini folded up the map and gave it to Dal, who put it in the glove compartment.

Half a mile or so up the road, Patty said, "There," and Mr. Sabatini turned off the road onto the desert floor. The truck bumped along in the dust. Wilbur was fanning his face with his hand.

"There," Patty said again.

"You sure you're not making this up?"

"Positive."

In a minute they came to signs that said PRIVATE, KEEP OUT! HIGH EXPLOSIVES! That sounded promising. In another minute they arrived at the top of a slight hill, and you could tell it was the right place because there were fresh tire marks everywhere. Mr. Sabatini stopped the truck, and they all got out and walked around. Dal slipped inside one of the deserted shacks and tried to open the front door, but it wouldn't budge, so he leaned out of a busted-out window and said, "Would anyone like to buy some uranium?"

There were several mine heads, from different eras, each surrounded by sections of hurricane fencing and hand-lettered signs that said: DANGEROUS. ABSOLUTELY NO TRESPASSING! LOOK OUT FOR SNAKES! Of these the most dangerous-looking was a vertical mine shaft that must have been equipped once with some kind of elevator for lowering the miners and raising the ore. Now it was just a deep, dark hole to nowhere. The kids stood with their fingers in the metal fence and tried to see in. If you tumbled down there, it'd be a while before you hit bottom. "Wilbur!" Mr. Sabatini said in his gym teacher's voice. "Leave that fence alone. We want to stay as a group."

CHAPTER 19

WHAT THEY FOUND INSTEAD

Wilbur was searching for pieces of silver the miners might have dropped. Patty sunned herself like a lizard on an outcropping of rock. Dal took giant steps with the Geiger counter, trying to see where the clicks were the loudest. Mr. Sabatini was exploring the original mine shaft, to see if it was safe for them all to go down.

Click-click-click. Dal lifted the box to his ear, but the sound was coming from someplace else, a dry, insistent *clicking* that seemed to fill the desert air. He watched as his stepfather hoisted himself out of the hole in a hurry.

"Dal?" Mr. Sabatini said. "Could you come here a minute, son?"

That was funny: he had never called him son before. What made Dal know that he should drop the Geiger counter and run?

Mr. Sabatini was sitting on the ground. "You'd better . . ." he said, smiling his trademark smile. "I've been bit by something. There it goes! There it goes! See if you can—no, Dal, let it go!"

At first it looked like a swollen hose, every part of it moving at once. Dal stood and watched its tapered neck and flat, triangular head, slightly lifted, as its body flowed over the dry ground.

He picked up a rock, held it high over his head, and brought it down with all his might—missed by a yard. Mr. Sabatini held up his leg like he was stretching out his calf muscle. Wilbur was there, panting.

"Gor," he said, "that monster's huge."

"Patty!" Dal shouted. "Get the doctor's bag." He grabbed a stick forked at one end. Chasing the snake—*do! don't!*—he lunged with a shiver that went all the way through him and pinned its ugly head. The rest of it—muscle—wrapped its body upward around the stick toward Dal's hand. "Help!" he screamed.

Wilbur Dunn and Patty Pucket came running from different directions. Patty lugged the doctor's bag in both hands. Was everybody screaming, or just Dal? Wilbur came staggering, slobber on his lips, his arms around a small boulder, which he heaved at the snake's flat head. Patty quickly stepped on the rock. "Get off," said Wilbur, pushing her and holding on to her at the same time. He jumped on the boulder, jumped and jumped, until the snake was a body, unmoving.

"He's dead," said Wilbur, cautiously moving the rock with his foot.

"Watch out for his head!" shouted Dal. "It might be still poisonous. Well, I don't know."

Mr. Sabatini was saying to Patty, "There's where he got me." He rolled his pants leg up, interested. "There, see?"

Two dots, hidden in his hair.

Patty opened the doctor's bag.

Mr. Sabatini closed his eyes and took a deep breath. "I feel dizzy," he said, and giggled. "A little sick, I'm afraid." He put his hand on the ground behind him, leaned away, and threw up something yellow.

"What should we do?" Dal cried, only it sounded fake.

Mr. Sabatini found Dal with his eyes and smiled at him. He looked tired. "Do you . . . have . . . a knife in there, Dal? Try cutting the skin . . . across the fang marks. You're supposed . . . to make little *x*'s. If you can, suck out some of the venom." He licked his dry lips. "S-sorry about this."

Patty unwrapped a green velvet pouch. Inside were three silver scalpels. She chose one and handed it to Dal. He looked at the knife. Mr. Sabatini's leg, where the bite was, had puffed up; the holes were tinier, almost white. He put the point of the scalpel on his stepfather's skin but couldn't bring himself to press down.

Patty said, "Here, give it to me." She put her tongue out of the side of her mouth and made two neat x's on Mr. Sabatini's leg. Enough blood seeped through to make the x's red. She leaned back, the scalpel still in her hand. Dal got down on his belly. He wriggled forward and put his mouth on Mr. Sabatini's hairy leg and sucked the salty blood.

"Gor," said Wilbur, the idiot.

"Don't swallow it." Mr. Sabatini's voice was a hoarse whisper.

Dal spit. He sucked and spit. On the ground was a pool of pink spit. He stopped to catch his breath. Patty was waiting with the medicine. Dal nodded, and she poured the whole bottle on Mr. Sabatini's leg. It stained the skin brown.

You're going to have to get me to town, Dal—only Mr. Sabatini hadn't said that or anything else. He had sagged sideways, his eyes half open.

Wilbur held his fists up and stamped his feet. "He's dead. Your daddy's dead."

"Shut up!" said Dal, jumping up and spitting again. He felt like socking Wilbur. Instead he carefully took hold of Mr. Sabatini's hands. They felt inert. He got a better grip and pulled with all his might, but all he managed to do was yank his stepfather's arms over his head.

"Get his feet," Dal said.

Patty used both hands to lift one of Mr. Sabatini's boots. Wilbur knelt down, took the other one under his arm, and struggled to stand up.

"Hurry," Dal said.

But there was no hurrying. Suspended by his hands and feet, the seat of his pants an inch off the ground, Mr. Sabatini was the heaviest thing in the world. They carried him six feet, then Patty dropped the foot she was carrying, and Mr. Sabatini slipped to the ground.

"He's too heavy," Wilbur said.

If you get bitten by a diamondback, you'd be better off with a shovel—to dig a hole with. By the time you get back to civilization, the venom will have spread. . . .

How much time had passed? Two minutes? Half an hour? How much time did a person have?

"Drag him!" said Dal. Wilbur wiped his hands on his pants and used them to grip one of Mr. Sabatini's hands. Dal took the other. "Patty, go let down the tailgate." She nodded once and ran ahead. The boys pulled with all their might, dragging Mr. Sabatini on the seat of his khaki pants, the heels of his boots leaving tracks in the dirt.

Patty was waiting in the back of the pickup truck, bent over like someone trying to touch her toes. She had managed to topple one of the bean sacks onto the ground. Squatting, she said, "Give me his hand."

Dal and Wilbur used all their strength to raise one of Mr. Sabatini's hands; the rest of him came with it. Patty fell out of the truck trying to get a good hold. She scrambled back in. Pulling from above, pushing from below, they at last got the unconscious man up into the bed of the truck, just barely. Patty lifted his foot clear, while Wilbur slammed the tailgate and Dal pinned it shut.

That was the easy part.

Patty put her hands in Mr. Sabatini's pockets. She handed his keys down to Dal. He looked at them. He didn't even know which one was the right one. Yes, he did. It said GM on it. He gave them to Wilbur. "This one. You drive. Quick! I'll read the map."

Wilbur batted the keys to the ground. "I don't know how to drive!"

"You can drive a tractor!"

"I can't drive no truck!"

Dal hated his guts. He picked up the keys. "You drive," he said to Patty.

"No, you," she said, momentarily putting her hand on his arm. "I'll tell you which way to turn."

"Wait," said Wilbur, running back toward the mine.

"Leave it!" Dal shouted. "Whatever it is! What the hell is he doing?" It didn't matter now if he said "hell."

"He must have left something. Come on." They got in the cab and slammed the doors.

"Wait!" cried Wilbur. He was galumphing back, holding the dead snake, still coiled around the stick, as far in front of himself as he could. When he reached the truck, he said, panting, "They're going to need that for the anti-venom serum. I read about it in *The Bite of the Snake Lady*."

"Good thinking," Dal said. "Toss it behind one of the bean sacks." In a friendly voice he added, "You ride back there, too, okay?"

"I ain't riding in the back with that." Wilbur came around to the other side and crowded Patty up against Dal.

Dal sat where Mr. Sabatini usually sat. He had to slide forward to touch the pedals. He wished he had paid more attention when his stepfather drove. Maybe it didn't matter. Maybe Mr. Sabatini had already died.

Dal jammed the key into the ignition, closed his eyes, and turned it. The truck jerked forward and back, dead.

Dal put his head on the steering wheel.

Patty hit him.

"You have to use the clutch," Wilbur said.

"Which one's the clutch?"

"The left one."

Dal reached with his leg and pressed the clutch pedal as far as it would go. He twisted the key again. This time the engine squealed, but—but it was running! Dal sat there, both hands on the steering wheel. The wheel itself was huge, but the part you held on to was skinny.

"Step on that one," Wilbur said, reaching across Patty to point. The engine went crazy. "Now let out the other one, you stupid moron."

The car lurched into motion. He was driving! He sat up tall to see.

He was driving, all right, headed straight for the mine shaft. Four hands on the wheel, his and Patty's, swung the car to the right.

"Shift it!" said Wilbur, leaning across Patty. "Step on the clutch again. I'll do it."

But Dal knew how to shift. Down is first, up and over is second, down is third.

They were going much too fast. Dal strained to see over the hood. He drove in circles, so as not to crash into the obstacles that lay all around.

"Which way do I go?" he screamed.

Patty sat on the edge of the seat. "There!" she said, pointing. "Go that way!" She helped turn the steering wheel. They went lickety-split down a bumpy road. Every once in a while a giant rock or straggly tree flew past. Dal's heart beat in his ears. He wanted to lean out the window and shout, "Mr. Sabatini—Dad—what do I do now?" A quiet voice said, *You know, you're not beaten till you think you are.* But glancing in the rearview mirror, all he could see was the shape that was his stepfather just lying there, one of his legs crammed against the tailgate, bouncing every time they hit a bump.

Dal held the steering wheel as tight as he could, determined not to veer off through the underbrush and onto the desert floor. The road went on an awfully long time. No one said anything.

"Look," said Wilbur. Dal glanced past the back of his head, out his open window. Up on the highway a huge truck steamed by.

"That's where we want to get to," said Patty, sitting back and crossing her arms.

But how did you get there? They stared through the windshield like kids at a drive-in.

"Turn!" shouted Wilbur. "Here!"

Dal swung the wheel in the direction Old Slobber was pointing, went *blang-blang* over a cattle guard, and drove into a field of black-eyed Susans. The road disappeared. The pickup truck stopped in the dirt. There were black-eyed Susans everywhere, waving, waving.

CHAPTER **20**

THE HOSPITAL

How Dal got the truck started again, backed over the cattle guard, found the highway that was going to Provo, Utah, he doesn't know to this day. What he does know is that once they were on the black-top, he drove like a bank robber in the getaway car. At the outskirts of the first town they came to, he didn't even slow down for a red light—Patty reached over, though, and honked the horn. Still, if a car had started across in front of them, they would have smashed into it and kept on going. Out of nowhere a police car appeared, its lights flashing.

"He's pointing to the side of the road," said Patty, twisting in her seat.

"He's gonna arrest you," said Wilbur, watching out the window. "You better put your hands up."

Dal stepped on the brake as hard as he could, and the truck stuttered to a stop. Before the policeman could squeeze out of his patrol car, the kids had jumped down from the pickup, all three talking at once.

Dal thought he heard Wilbur crying, then realized *he* was. Once the policeman understood what had happened, he radioed for help. For a long, stupid minute everybody just stood there.

"You drive that pickup?" the policeman said, looking down at Dal.

"Yes, sir." He wondered if he really should put his hands up.

From a great distance, drawing nearer, a siren wailed through the afternoon. A gleaming white ambulance that nothing could stop slid around the corner. Two men in jackets jumped out. They didn't even stop to talk to the policeman but went straight to the back of the truck and gently lowered the tailgate. Mr. Sabatini fell with it, but one of the attendants pinned his body with his own, while the other ran to get the stretcher. "That the mother who bit him?" he said calmly to the policeman. The lights from the ambulance cast a red wash on the street.

"Looks like it."

"Shoot, that's a diamondback. She's responsible for more fatalities than any other snake around here."

The policeman, with his arms stretched wide, escorted the children over to his car. Someone was saying something on his car radio. It crackled. He picked up the microphone and said something back. Dal wondered if he would have to go to jail right away for driving underage. The policeman said, "Get in, kids." To Dal he said, "That your daddy?" Dal nodded. "You better sit up front with me." So Dal slid onto the big seat, swiveling his head to see what was happening outside. They were slamming the doors to the ambulance. First the lights swooped; then the sirens went *whyee, whyee.* Patty's clammy hand came over the seat and patted his shoulder. The policeman reached up and switched his lights on, too. He pulled in front of the ambulance. They drove together through town in a convoy of two. People on the sidewalk stood watching. On the outskirts of town was a brand-new hospital, standing all by itself in an empty field of dirt and weeds. They followed the blue sign that said EMERGENCY. Even before the ambulance had come to a complete stop, the rear door opened, and one of the attendants jumped out. The stretcher had wheels, and they ran with it through the automatic doors.

Dal and Wilbur and Patty followed the policeman, who had on a black leather jacket even though it was hot out. A nurse met them in the lobby. "You all better sit down. I have to ask you some important questions."

They sat in colored plastic chairs.

"Was that the snake that bit him?" the nurse said. "You're sure? Do you know how old your dad is? What type of blood he has? Has he ever had snake antivenin before?"

Dal racked his brains. He didn't know Mr. Sabatini's age or blood type. He didn't think he had ever had antivenin before.

"Are you his children?"

Wilbur wanted to answer some of the questions, too. "We ain't his children," he said. "He is." He pointed to Dal. "I wish I was, though."

"I am," Dal said.

The policeman loomed over their shoulders. "What kind of pop you kids like?"

"R. C.," said Wilbur.

"Dr. Pepper, please," said Patty.

"I don't care," said Dal. "Anything's fine."

In a minute the policeman was back. "I bought you some salty peanuts." He poured some in each of their outstretched hands.

"Thanks," the children said in unison.

"How old are you anyway?" the policeman asked, squatting down behind them.

Patty said, "I'm eleven."

"I'm twelve, and he's eleven," said Wilbur.

"Is my dad going to be all right?" Dal asked, tears burning the insides of his eyes.

The policeman looked at the nurse, and the nurse smiled. She hugged Dal. "It's too early to tell, honey."

Dal was walking around outside. He wanted to be alone, so

Wilbur and Patty sat on the curb next to the emergency sign. They were squabbling about something: you could hear their voices but not what they were saying. Behind the hospital were mounds of building material. Dal walked past them into a stand of dusty trees. He knew the names of some of them. That's an aspen, he said to himself, picking a jagged leaf off a branch. A hidden brook ran through the clutter of trees and weeds. Unhooking branches from in front of his face, Dal walked beside the brook a ways.

As he walked, he stood as straight as he could. The problem was that if he didn't think about his posture, his shoulders naturally drooped. But he would remember from now on if it killed him. He wished he could throw better and catch better, like Jimmy Beard. Mr. Sabatini had said once, "That boy's headed for the majors." He wished he wasn't so shy. Just a few days before, on Main Street, he had bumped into Mrs. Turner, who was coming out of the dry-goods store. Dal pretended he was Mr. Sabatini. Lifting his hat and grinning, he said, "Hello there, Mrs. Turner."

Mrs. Turner looked surprised, but she smiled back and said, "Why, hello there, junior."

He would learn to do all the things Mr. Sabatini could do: play ball and camp out and talk to people. And eat stinky cheese and mayonnaise. And be nice to Kate, who wasn't that bad for a five-year-old.

Although they lived on different planets, Mr. Sabatini liked him—he was sure of it. When he was going to run an errand, he'd say, "Come on, Dal. Keep me company." And he'd laugh when Dal said some of the things that popped into his head—it was surprised laughter. Sometimes his jokes weren't even that funny. Like the time Mr. Sabatini tried to revive a dried-up cactus plant they'd found along the highway, and Dal wrote on a piece of paper, "I'M DEAD, SORRY." His stepdad roared with laughter, and afterward—after the cactus plant had been dumped in the trash—Dal found the note, neatly folded, in one of his stepdad's *Reader's Digest*s.

Back in June Dal wasn't even sure he wanted to go out West with Mr. Sabatini. But if he hadn't followed him onto the train, he never would have gotten to stay at the Garden of Eden Motel. He never would have met Patty and Wilbur or learned to rogue or ridden a horse or bought shares in a uranium mine. He might never have found out what Mr. Sabatini was really like.

Dal ran as fast as he could. Patty's small voice was shouting, "Dal!" Wilbur was waving his arms over his head. Dal ran and cried and prayed all at the same time. "Please, God," he said out loud, "don't let anything bad happen to Hercules 'Harry' Sabatini." He said his whole name, so God would know who he meant, but then he added, "To my dad."

"What?" he called when he was within shouting distance of Wilbur.

"They want to talk to you," both his friends said together.

The doctor's name was Dr. Young. He was tall and chubby and had thick glasses. "I wanted to shake your hand," he said. "All three of you. You probably saved this man's life."

Dal didn't say anything; he just looked at the doctor.

"Come on. He's been asking for you. He wants to see you."

Patty hung back, but Wilbur said, "Can I come, too?"

"Sure," said Dr. Young. "You can all come."

They followed the doctor through a maze of corridors. The doors were brand-new and still smelled like pine trees. The door to his dad's room was open. A different nurse was coming out, carrying a pile of sheets. She smiled at Dal. He couldn't help smiling back.

Mr. Sabatini was sitting up in bed with a tray on his lap.

"He's still weak," the doctor said in a low voice, but to Dal he looked the same as ever. Dal and Mr. Sabatini didn't touch that much except when they shook hands, but this time Dal ran to his bed and put his head on his chest and wrapped his arms around him. Mr. Sabatini smelled like medicine.

He said in a funny whisper, "There's room for more," and somehow Wilbur's and Patty's heads were there, too. He wasn't even their stepfather.

"We want to keep an eye on him for a day or two, but he should be fine. That was a close call, Mr. Sabatini. With snakebites time is of the essence."

They hung around as long as they could. Patty told Dr. Young she wanted to be a doctor someday. "You will," Dr. Young prophesied. "You will."

"Girls can't be doctors," Wilbur said, guffawing. "You can be a nurse."

Patty put her hands on her hips. "Can, too. I can be anything I want to be."

"I'm going to be a ambulance driver," Wilbur said.

Dal was spinning on a swivel chair. Dr. Young asked him what he was going to be. He couldn't say "cowboy" out West. "A writer." What made him say that?

Mr. Sabatini couldn't keep his eyes open, but the doctor said that was normal. "I gave him a sedative. Let's let him get some sleep, shall we?"

They went back down the corridor. Wilbur was getting on Dal's nerves. He wanted to tell him to stand up straight. He called home from a pay phone in the lobby. The operator said, "What number, please?"

Dal felt grown-up. For once he knew the answer. "I want to call Detroit, Michigan, and reverse the charges." After he gave the number, the operator said she'd call him back, so he hung up and waited. When the phone rang, he jumped. Before he could say, "Hello?" his mom was saying, "Harry, what's happened? Is Dal all right?"

"It's me," he said.

"What's happened, darling?" His mom was from Virginia and always called him "darling."

"Dad got bit by a snake. A diamondback, four feet long. Wilbur killed it, and Patty cut his leg with a silver scalpel. I drove him to the hospital. He's okay, though," he added. He told her all the details—well, not all of them. He didn't say anything about the uranium mine.

She didn't entirely believe him when he said that everything was fine, so he handed the phone to Patty and went to look for Dr. Young, who was in the emergency room. When they got back, Patty was talking to Dal's mom as though she had known her all her life.

"He's all right," Dr. Young said into the phone. He said, "That's quite some boy you've got there."

That night, at the nurse's house—she had a little boy who followed them everywhere—Dal dreamed that he met Dwight D. Eisenhower down by the lake. Dal didn't know if he should call him Mr. President or just plain Ike. At first Ike didn't say anything. He just reached back and cast his fishing line over the water. Then, as he was reeling it back in, he said, "I heard about your achievement."

That's when Dal noticed that there was someone else there, too, a young soldier, leaning against a jeep.

Dal couldn't take his eyes off him. Where had he seen that face before? "Patty and Wilbur helped, too," he said.

The young soldier smiled.

When Dal woke up, he shook Wilbur's shoulder and told him about the dream. But Wilbur didn't believe it was really the President and kept trying to trip him up with questions like "What was he wearing?" Dal didn't say who else he had seen and that he looked just like he did in the photograph.

When Dal's dad got out of the hospital two days later, he drove the hundred or so miles back to the Garden of Eden Motel, first dropping Patty off at the Fosters'. "See you, Dal," she said, waving. "See you, Mr. Sabatini. See you, Wilbur."

Wilbur got off under the East-of-Eden Ranch sign. They waited until he had lugged his suitcase out of the back. "I had a good time," he said. Mr. Sabatini reached out his window and shook the boy's hand.

GOING HOME

They spent the rest of July and the first two weeks of August doing the same old work. Most days Dal went along to keep his stepdad company. On weekends, whenever possible, they went on camping trips, once hitchhiking all the way to Yellowstone National Park— but that's another story. Except for a slight red mark on his shin, you couldn't tell that Mr. Sabatini had ever been bitten by a deadly snake. He was good as new.

When they finished their work out West, they packed their bags and said good-bye to everybody. Somebody must have driven them to the station in Pocatello, where they boarded the train that took them home, but all that is a blur in Dal's mind: the return train ride, being met at the station in downtown Detroit. At first he was glad to be home, but then he didn't have anything to do, it was hot and muggy, and school started in less than two weeks.

As time passed, it got harder and harder to believe that any of this had really happened. All he had for a souvenir was a small Indian drum, his gift to Kate. When the feathers fell off and the leather cracked and came apart, he found that there was a tin can underneath. He had his rocks, neatly labeled and set upon the shelves where he used to keep his toys. Each week he would put a different rock on the table beside his bed. He liked to stare at it in the glow from his nightlight as he fell asleep. His dad let him keep the stock certificate to the uranium mine. Amazingly, the mine really did produce some uranium, though not enough to pay a dividend. Dal wondered if Patty ever got any money from it. The uranium mine became a family joke.

For a while Dal had a photo album of his trip to Idaho. Mr. Sabatini had bought him a Kodak Brownie camera, sort of as a reward for driving him to the hospital, though he never said so in so many words. In his last week out West Dal went around taking pictures of everything he could think of: the motel, the roguing crew, the Fosters' yard. Unfortunately, during one of their many moves, the photo album disappeared.

Except for one picture, slightly concave from being kept under his pillow for so long. In it Jerry and Margaret Foster are standing in front of a pickup truck with Patty between them. Mr. Foster is smiling down at Sheppy, who is standing on his hind legs with his front paws stretched up to his master's belt. Mrs. Foster is talking to someone over the head of the cameraman, Mr. Sabatini probably. Patty is looking right at the camera. Her mouth is slightly open, the beginning of a smile on her face.

Seconds after the picture was taken, when Dal's dad and Mr. Foster were yakking about something and Mrs. Foster had gone into the house for a minute, Dal nonchalantly stepped up to Patty and kissed her on her cheek. It felt firmer and more ordinary than he had expected. He had been thinking about doing it for three whole days, practicing on the muscle of his arm. If she was planning to slap him, she never got the chance. Before she or anybody else could make a move, Dal had cleared an irrigation ditch and was galloping across the pasture toward the open sky.

DATE DUE

NOV 2 8 2002			

FOLLETT